Black Swan

Black Swan

Farrukh Dhondy

Houghton Mifflin Company
Boston 1993

Library of Congress Cataloging-in-Publication Data

Dhondy, Farrukh.
  Black swan / Farrukh Dhondy.
    p. cm.
  Summary: While taking care of an elderly man, Rose realizes that
they are being watched, and becomes caught up in a mystery going
back to Elizabethan England involving Shakespeare, Marlow, and an
extraordinary black slave.
  ISBN 0-395-66076-9
  [1. Mystery and detective stories.   2. England — Fiction.
3. Marlowe, Christopher, 1564–1593 — Fiction.   4. Shakespeare,
William, 1564–1616 — Fiction.   5. Blacks — England — Fiction.
6. Homosexuality — Fiction.]   I. Title.
PZ7.D5414B1   1993
[Fic] — dc20   92-30425
                               CIP
                               AC

Printed in the United States of America

BP   10   9   8   7   6   5   4   3   2   1

Black Swan

ROSE WAS DANCING with the devils when she heard the laughter break out. The stroboscope made the shadows jump in blue light at sickening speed. It was the signal to begin the fiendish laughter, and she laughed with the rest of them. Ha. The actors held hands and formed a ring. Above them the skeletons, hung with flat-sounding bells, jangled. The dragons appeared on the platform breathing fire through the backdrops. The music rose. She'd done this a hundred times in rehearsals but it sounded louder than ever before and more piercing in her ears. The stroboscope flashed on and off and made her feel just a little sick, like being in the back of a car whose engine drones and makes your bones vibrate.

Then it all went silent and she couldn't remember exactly where she was or what she was supposed to do. The audience began tittering. One of the boys, a devil who was dancing opposite, was making faces at her. She was trying to read his lips but knew it was hopeless. Her mind was blank except for the thought "my mind is a blank." She took her mask off. The audience was laughing now and she heard the sound of ten prompts, from the prompter, from the wings, from the other actors. Rose was a statue. Disaster. It was like one of those dreams in which you catch yourself heading for a crash.

Rose was wishing for the words to come back. She looked at the audience, darkness, no faces except for a few shining foreheads. The laugh rose, first one then a cloud, like a lot of light helium balloons, into the Gothic arches and recesses of the hall, out of the pointed windows which were open for this summer night. She had stopped.

The ring of devils was still moving but her feet had given up. She could feel them, but she wasn't in control.

It seemed an eternity. The voices, the prompts around her, became louder. Yes, now she remembered only that she'd forgotten. Her stomach felt knotted.

Then the lines came. It was obvious, all the devils were hissing the line together. Charles had begun it and they had taken it up and were hissing it in chorus, reminding her of her lines. "My God, my God, look not so fierce on me."

That was it. She screamed the line and the audience's laughter was lost in the scream. She was safe, she remembered.

"Adders and serpents, let me breathe awhile."

The devils had moved to the shadows of the stage and Rose was now alone by the footlights, completely in command. She felt the sweat from under her arms trickle down the side of her bra. She was safe.

"Ugly hell, gape not, come not, Lucifer!
I'll burn my books. Ah, Mephostophilis!"

Somehow, on automatic pilot she got to the end of the play and as they applauded, Rose felt cheated of the joy of acting.

Some funny part of her brain had taken over and recranked her memory.

The audience clapped and clapped, till the cast returned three times to take a bow. Then Miss Carr, the drama teacher, dropped the curtain and ran up to Rose.

"Are you all right?"

"Yes."

"What happened?"

"I don't know. I must have forgotten my . . ."

"Doesn't matter, you look very pale. Come and sit down."

Miss Carr held on to Rose and led her away from the green-room through the corridor to the Head's study.

"You can sit here. I'll get you some water. Do you feel okay?"

"My head's going round a bit, that's all."

"Has your mother come?"

Rose nodded.

"I'll tell her where you are. It was fantastic."

"Miss, I'm sorry," Rose said as Miss Carr left.

"Don't be silly."

She didn't want to be in the headmaster's study. She looked round. She'd been in this room once when she was interviewed after she'd won the scholarship. It was an oak-paneled study with bookshelves and a huge painting of a man being burnt at the stake.

Her mother came into the room and then the headmaster, Mr. Crofton Page.

"You all right, darling?" her mother asked.

"I am sorry, sir," Rose muttered.

"It was a strikingly good performance. I am sorry you don't feel well, but it was magnificent, a triumph. If you forgot a line or two, well, the devil take the lines. Perhaps he did!"

"I don't know what happened, sir," Rose said.

"Are you well enough to join the others? A drop of sherry for the leavers?"

"No, I think I'll go home, sir." Rose didn't want to face the others.

"When the parents have dispersed I'll drive you home myself. Do sit down Mrs. Hassan, it's lovely to see you again," said Mr. Page.

When he left the room, Rose said, "I feel fine now, Mom, can't we take the bus?"

She wanted to avoid Mr. Page. She'd apologized. The rest of the cast would come to get her. They'd be in the corridor even now, but she wanted to be alone. With Mom.

Rose looked at the door. She knew what her mother was going to say next, the words would tumble out of her, and Rose didn't want anyone else to hear them.

"Mom don't," she protested. "Just don't mention money and what we can afford and all this . . ."

"But we can't afford a taxi and I'm not having you waiting at the bus stop . . ."

"All right. I'll go in the car. Please, not in the headmaster's office."

"No shame in it," her mother said, and took a cushion off the headmaster's chair and tried to put it behind Rose's back.

"Mom, please, just put it back."

"What happened? You must've felt faint."

"I don't know what happened, do I?" Rose said in the tone she knew would put her mother off further questioning.

4

Mr. Page came in. "Better? Sure you won't stay?"

"I think we'd better go, sir."

"Ready when you are, Mrs. Hassan," he said. He had a bunch of car keys in his hand and he jingled them.

"I'm fine," Rose said and began to walk to the door. She wanted to get it over with. Outside in the corridor, as she expected, there were several of the actors and Miss Carr. Rose didn't want to speak to them; she just wanted to get home. The boys had brought her a bunch of flowers. She took them and smiled. Mr. Page, gauging her mood, said they would no doubt meet again at school reunions and that he had tried to persuade her to stay but perhaps she'd better go and rest.

Rose knew that if she agreed to stay for the party her mother would be persuaded, too, and she didn't want to be the only one with a mother at their farewell do. What the headmaster said was probably true. She would meet them after the summer holidays or come across them somewhere in London when most of them got back from their holidays and jaunts. She know some of them were going abroad, in pairs, and some were going with their parents. She would stay in London and work. The talk at the party would be all about going abroad and university entrances and she didn't particularly want to discuss the fact that she would stay and help her mother out and try to save some money over the summer holidays.

The Head drove them home in his large estate car. Rose sat next to him and her mother sat in the back and told him where to turn.

"Will Mr. Hassan be back for the summer? He's in the Navy isn't he, if I remember rightly, Rose?"

"Oh, I doubt it," Mrs. Hassan said.

"So there's only Rose and yourself?"

Rose wondered whether he was entitled to ask these questions. He was the headmaster, but she felt he wasn't making polite conversation, he somehow really wanted to know.

"I'm very proud of you," he turned to Rose. "You mustn't forget us altogether. You have got your provisional admission to university, haven't you?"

"And to drama school, sir."

"Oh yes, Central, wasn't it?"

"Yes, sir."

Suppose the people who had offered her scholarships to these drama colleges heard that she'd made a fool of herself in a school production of *Doctor Faustus*?

"You know, Rose, I'm not in the least surprised at your losing step during the play. It's a very odd thing. It's happened before. Every time the school decides to do Marlow's *Faustus* there's some kind of small disaster. I remember eight years ago, the green-room caught fire. A few curtains got burnt. And in the school record there's always been some small goings-on. I told Miss Carr but she's an atheist, you know, doesn't believe in God or the devil."

"But she is superstitious, she won't let us say 'Macbeth' when we're in drama because it brings bad luck. We have to say 'The Scottish Play.' "

They stepped out of the car. The Head held the door for her mother and he wished them a "happy holiday." He didn't seem to mind where they lived, though Rose felt slightly embarrassed when her mother directed him through the side streets and in through the gates of the estate. None of the other kids at her posh school lived on a council estate.

The first time Rose went to the school the Head had talked to her for two hours. He had asked questions. She was just a

6

silly little kid then. She'd won the scholarship and her mother had dressed her in her new blazer and her new skirt and walked with her to the bus stop.

"Martyr's" was what the locals called the school and all over England it had acquired that name, though Rose was not to know because she mixed in a society that did not know or care about the nicknames of private schools.

The school's actual name was Cranmer, Latimer and Ridley College, sometimes abbreviated to CLR. It was some way from Brixton where they lived.

Rose's mother unlocked the door to their flat on the third floor.

"Now you lie down, I'll get you a cup of tea."

"Don't fuss, Mom, I don't need to lie down."

"I liked the play; it was lovely, really lovely."

"That's the wrong word to use," Rose said. She wanted to be alone. She wanted to look at the script again. The way her mother said "lovely" really irritated her. She found her mother understood less and less of what she was doing, thinking, the sort of arguments she wanted to have with her. And yet they were close.

With her teachers and with a few of her schoolmates she could argue and talk through ideas. With her mother it was always niggling matters of fact; her mother was as stubborn as an ink stain. She would never admit that she didn't know this or that fact, hadn't read the books that Rose read. When Rose mentioned a play, her mother would say she had read it long ago and couldn't remember it. She had too much work now to think of plays.

"He used to read plays." Her mother never used her father's name. He was still on that voyage as far as they knew.

Rose didn't remember much about him, only his name and that he had been a painter once and then a sign painter. One day he went to visit a friend in Liverpool and came back to tell her mother that he had joined the merchant navy and was going away to sea for six months. He'd returned. Then he'd gone again, and then again after Rose was born. Each time he returned with no money, looking thinner, wiser, more angry with the world.

"More angry with me, and after you were born, with you. There was no reasoning with the brute." Her mother had converted to Islam when they were first married and joined the small Muslim community in Cardiff. And when there were not enough signs to paint in Cardiff they had come to London. "He had friends all over the world. Never lacked a friend to lead him astray," Mother would say.

There was nothing left of Merry Hassan in their London flat. Maybe a photograph or two in Mom's old album, his name which they both carried and the ghost of his blackness. The fact of color, differentness, which Rose inherited in her complexion. It was a constant reminder of this missing dad.

He had of course left her a legacy, if indeed he was dead, of his color. Rose was darkish skinned and she had curly brown hair and green eyes. Even as a child she knew that shop assistants, policemen, milkmen, would look from her to her mother and wonder. The schoolteachers would look from her to her mother and pretend they were not wondering.

That night Rose's mother turned in early. She had to wake up and go to work early the next morning. Rose usually watched the news and a documentary or drama on television, but she decided to get to bed too.

Now she was dying to reread the part of the play, Scene XIX, in which she had been struck dumb.

She could recall the feeling. It wasn't embarrassment. It wasn't forgetfulness. She knew the lines really well. Her tongue couldn't speak the words, her mind couldn't think them. And the words were "My God."

How could she have stumbled into that blankness? Rose wasn't superstitious, but it was a play about a man selling his soul to the devil. She didn't believe in devils. She kept the light on and tried to sleep, leaving a couple of books open on top of her duvet so that if Mom asked in the morning why the lights were still on, she could say she dropped off while reading.

Though she turned away from it, the light wouldn't let Rose sleep. She got up and made sure there was no chink of darkness peering through the curtains of the window which overlooked the central court of her estate. She lay awake and the memory of the darkened stage came back to her though she tried to put it out of her mind. She was most worried by the fact that she had frozen on stage. Not a good thing for someone who wanted to make a career of acting. Rose had always been the drama teacher's pet. In this very production she had been cast as a man because of her acting ability. Miss Carr said she was more convincing than any of the boys, and Miss Carr wanted to experiment with the notion that women, too, could sell their souls to the devil. It was weird but even the boys accepted it. After a while. Rose knew that Charles wanted to play Faust. He too had applied to drama schools and was waiting for his results, but then he was given the better part of the devil.

She thought she'd never sleep, not that night, not ever again, but realized she had when the sound of her mother in

9

the kitchen woke her up. The first thought that struck Rose was that she was being warned. Maybe something was wrong with the fact that she had played Faust. The Gods of the stage didn't like it. Gods of the stage? Ridiculous! Absurd. She called out to her mother.

There was no answer. She looked at the time. It was only three in the morning. Mom didn't have to be up till six. She heard her coughing. A low growl of a cough which got louder. Then she heard her mom retching. She wasn't in the kitchen, she was in the bathroom.

Rose got up and ran to the bathroom. He mother was kneeling next to the toilet bowl and she was vomiting blood. A thin red stream of blood and what seemed like very thin saliva came steadily, slowly, out of her mouth.

"What happened? Oh my God," Rose said, and panic seized her. Mom was never sick.

"I'll call the ambulance," Rose said and her mother nodded and her head dropped on to the edge of the toilet bowl. Rose didn't wait to lift her up. She must get help. She went out on to the walkway and banged at the door of their neighbor's flat.

She could hear her neighbor's anxious voice asking who it was, clearing his throat.

"It's me, Rose," she shouted.

Mr. Habib Ullah opened the door. He was wearing a cloth around his waist and his hairy belly stuck out over it. Behind him Rose could see Rahim, their teenage son, with a stick. They must have thought it was some sort of threat, the urgent knock and her shouting.

"Rosey, what is happened?"

"My mother, she's ill. Can you call an ambulance?"

"What happened to her?" Mr. Ullah asked, but he was already halfway to the phone on the table in the hall. He shouted in Bengali for his wife and children to wake up and go to Rose's assistance.

Rose rushed back. Her mother had fallen unconscious on the bathroom floor and as she breathed there was a low gurgling sound from her throat.

All day Rose was at the hospital. They operated immediately on her mother and she was unconscious when Rose was allowed back to her bedside.

The doctors wouldn't let Rose stay all night at the hospital. The young doctor explained that they didn't know what had caused a massive ulceration in her mother's abdomen, but something had burst and it would take weeks or months, under medical supervision, to heal.

"Is there anyone else at home?" the doctor asked.

"Yes, Dad's there," Rose lied. She didn't want this doctor poking his snooty nose into their business.

"Well, can you tell him we'd like to see him? As soon as possible?"

Rose knew she'd have to return to face this doctor the next day.

"He won't come," she said. "Tell you the truth, he doesn't believe in hospitals and doctors. He's a Witness, a Jehovah's Witness, and thinks God's will must prevail and doctors are meddling . . . er, I don't believe that, I called the ambulance, my brothers and I, we can believe what we want."

"Are they older brothers?"

"No, no, younger, but my aunt can come and look after everybody. And I can."

The doctor looked at her and was perhaps about to question her further, but dropped it. He just nodded and left the ward.

At first Rose was terrified to be in the flat alone. She didn't sleep. She couldn't quite decide what had happened or what she should do about it. As soon as she relaxed she felt the tears come to her eyes. She didn't fight them, but let them fall. There was no aunt and there were no relatives. Mom worked for her living looking after an old man. The old man, Mr. Bernier, paid her very well.

At about seven the next morning the phone rang. Rose thought it must be the hospital and her stomach tightened with anticipation.

Silence at first at the other end when she picked up the phone.

"Martha, I say, Martha, what the hell has gone wrong with you man, I've been starving here for thirty-six hours and . . ."

The voice was old and feeble. Petulant. Rose had never spoken to Mr. Bernier before. Her mother said very little about him. She had worked for him for years now and she always said that Rose shouldn't mention him to anyone.

How could she have forgotten about Mr. Bernier? She knew that he depended on her mother alone to look after him. There were other men in the house. That was evident from what her mother said about the job, but they were detectives or policemen or something.

"This is not Martha, sir, this is her daughter, Rose."

"Well get me Martha, nuh man, what are you impersonating people for?"

"She's in the hospital, sir," Rose said.

"Oh God, what the hell for? What does she think I'll do for breakfast?"

Mom often seemed terrified of the old man but Rose had never found out why.

"I'm sorry you are suffering, sir," Rose said, "I'm sure if my mother could come and help you out, she would."

"You are sorry, child? Sorry? Don't just be sorry, man, come and sort this mess out."

"What me, sir?"

"Yes you, this thing is in the family. Your mother told me about you. You better come soon."

The old man put the phone down.

Her mother wouldn't be allowed visitors at the hospital till the afternoon. The old man would pay her. It was a relief. Rose had never been to the house but she knew where her mother kept the address and phone number.

Rose dressed and crossed the forecourt of the estate and went through the little park at the end of it. A gang of young men, mostly black, were, even at that time of the morning, playing volleyball. They were wearing track suits. Though it was the beginning of summer, it was cold and their breath went up in white wisps as they shouted. They knew her and she them. They called out to her.

"Looking fit!"

She didn't reply but kissed the air in their direction.

"Tonight is the night," another said. "You and me, Rose petal!"

"Thorns too," Rose said.

"Eh, hold on guy, Rosey wha' happen to your mother?" one of them asked.

"Operation, I don't know yet."

"Tell her love from me ya? And get well soon and thing."

"Thanks, Granger, I'll tell her."

"Is she all right to go see her in the hospital?"

"Not yet, but she'll be okay, I hope."

Rose was met at the door by the man whom her mother referred to as the Inspector.

He was expecting her.

"You are Rose? Mr. Bernier tells me you are going to look after him for a few days while your mother is in the hospital?"

Oh really? Rose thought. She hadn't made up her mind yet. She had known throughout this last year that she would have to get a summer job. They had no savings and, unlike the rest of the kids in her class, Rose couldn't afford to take up the offers of travel fellowships and grants that Miss Carr had suggested she try for. She knew that she would have to get some money together. If the worst came to the worst, she would go to work in some fast food place. She had been told that she would have to lie to get the job. They didn't want people who were just about to go to university. So she'd have to say she was on the job market. Now that Mom was in the hospital, they'd need more money than a fast food job would pay.

The Inspector didn't wait for her to reply. He shut the door behind her and led her through the hallway and then bounded up the stairs. He was a young man, tall and thin and the first thing Rose noticed about him was his adam's apple, which bobbed up and down as he spoke, and his slightly hooded eyes. What was odd about him? Rose thought and as she followed him up the stairs she knew; his head was too small for his height.

The Inspector stopped at the top of the stairs.

"Just refer to me as John. I'm one of Mr. Bernier's helpers. But I'm not always here. There's somebody here in the day and one person sleeps here at night. Sometimes I come and go. Your mother's told you that Mr. Bernier is not to be talked about. What did she tell you about him?"

"That he's eighty-two but doesn't have false teeth."

"Good. What else?"

"Nothing much. He has a three-and-a-half minute boiled egg at seven every morning, and if it's late or if it's overdone or underdone, then he shouts."

"That's good too. If you know all that, you'll soon get used to his ways. Now before we go in, how good are you at reading and writing?"

"I can read and write. English, that is," said Rose.

"Don't start fancying yourself as a comedian. He asked me to ask you, see? It's some work your mother couldn't do, so he's quite excited about the possibility, you know what I mean?"

The Inspector hesitated before the door to the bedroom at the top of the stairs. He looked again at Rose, up and down.

"Look, we could have given your mother and you a lot of tall stories. But she's a wonderful lady and you're a mature girl. Mr. Bernier is in some danger. You can't go talking about him or me or where the house is or anything. I think you understand. Use your mother's key — do you have it?"

Rose nodded. John knocked at the door, said he'd see her in a day or two and bounded down the stairs, taking them three at a time like a little boy who'd challenged himself to do it.

Mr. Bernier was tall and his curly hair tight on his head had turned stark white. It looked quite startling, Rose thought, against his black skin. He had a thin sharp nose. He wore jeans and a sweatshirt. There was an air of agelessness about him.

"You are Rose?" He crossed the room and shook her hand.

"Your mother has been so good to me, so I knew you'd be an angel too."

Rose noted that the accent was distinctly Oxford or posh of some sort, with a tinge of West Indian somewhere. Definitely not American and not African.

"Your mother tells me you're studying literature."

Rose said she was.

"And how is she?" asked the old man. It was obviously an afterthought. Rose tested the curiosity behind the question by not answering. The old man didn't seem to notice.

The room in which they stood was a study and Rose could see that next to it, through a small arch, was the old man's bedroom. The study had a sloping roof with a skylight and large windows overlooking the back garden which was well tended and ended in a high wall. The room was lined with bookshelves. As Rose found later there were manuscripts and trunkloads of books everywhere in the house and they were labeled with numbers as though they had been moved from somewhere else. In the study there was an oak desk and a table, presumably for her, and two typewriters and pens and paper.

"It's not just typing. I can type myself but the wrist hasn't healed yet. An accident."

Rose noticed the right hand was under a rather fancy-looking leather stirrup, buttoned up and leaving the fingers loose.

"I want you to do research, looking up things. Your mother couldn't do it. I am delighted to have a woman of your talents."

Rose was flattered just by his voice, and by the fact that an old man could say this kind of thing to her. But she was suspicious. He might be the sort of person who would give her grand ideas and use her as a menial, really push her around.

"Now that your poor mother has been taken ill, I'll pay her a recovery wage, and since you are going to do much more for me, I'll pay you twice what I pay her. Is that any good to you? I want to get these money matters out of the way, man. I would have asked the feller to speak to you about cash, but then I thought I'd do it myself. We don't want the likes of the Inspector knowing our business, eh?" He was instantly familiar. That was a very generous offer, Rose thought. It was three times what she had expected. A shadow of a doubt crossed her mind. If he was paying her all that much, what extraordinary things would he want her to do?

"You surely accept that, don't you?"

"Yes, of course, and thank you, Mr. Bernier. From me and Mom."

On the first day and the day after, Mr. B asked her to move pieces of paper, to check the numbers of pages in manuscripts, to look through books and mark things.

"I am working on something and you have to help," the old man said. He asked her to look through all the books on the small table in the corner. They were biographies of seventeenth century playwrights, three biographies of Shakespeare and two of Christopher Marlowe. "It's a nuisance when the books don't have an index, you see. What I want you to do is read through this book" — he picked up a life of Shake-speare with a thick black cover — "and I want you to mark in green every time the name Marlowe is mentioned and mark in red any other names of playwrights and people of the time. Only the names."

Marlowe. Her mother couldn't have told him about her fainting on stage, but she may have mentioned that Rose was acting in a school play. Knowing her mother, she would have boasted about it.

Rose said she knew who Marlowe was and that she had got into trouble while taking part in a performance of one of his plays.

Mr. B was interested.

"You defied the director? No, you threw furniture about. Let me guess. I knew a feller who flung benches at the audience because he thought they were about to boo him and throw tomatoes or chairs at him. He ruined his performance and misjudged the audience. But he got famous, man. For throwing furniture at the front rows. Created a lot of excitement."

"I don't know what happened. It's just silly."

"The play or you?"

"Me."

"You must tell me, then."

"I . . . I couldn't finish it. I froze up. I couldn't remember my lines."

"That's not uncommon. I knew a fine actress once, American. She fainted in the middle of playing Cleopatra. The audience was ignorant but expected her to die so they rose to their feet and clapped and Antony had to improvise. Anyway, what was your play?"

"*Doctor Faustus.*"

Mr. Bernier's shoulders came forward. He looked at Rose. For a few moments he said nothing. Then he asked her to get a book from the shelves. He knew where it was. It would be along to the left on the fifth shelf down.

She handed it to him and he turned the pages, ignoring her. He shut the book.

"That play," he said, "I am not a superstitious man, but when they played it in the seventeenth and in the eighteenth and again in the nineteenth centuries, they used to light up the stage and if I remember right, there was a dragon in the setting and the public who went to see it saw devils. One feller, great actor of his time, James Alleyn, he was in the play and he saw real devils coming for him. Helluva business, child. People say these things. They write them down." He patted the book.

He wanted to ask her what exactly had happened. She could see the question in his eyes but he didn't ask. Instead he asked about her mother. Very sincere now.

"You mustn't fear for money. We have enough." The old man gave Rose an envelope.

"Put it away and count it later. Careful with it."

Later on, when she was walking by the wall of the large house in Forest Hill towards the bus stop, she counted the money. Three hundred pounds. For her. The month's wages? The week's wages? She didn't know. It was funny the way he said "we" have enough.

"Do you know your way around London?"

"Yes, Mr. B, why?" Rose said. (She had hit upon this formula, calling him "Mr. B" instead of "sir," but she wasn't totally sure of this form of address. Sometimes she just left an awkward pause at the end of what she was saying, a blank where the "sir" should have been.)

"Because I want to send you somewhere. Something is bothering me and you are the one. You can do it. Take a book, an exercise book, or some sheets of paper. Take a pen or pencil. I want you to go to a place I shall direct you to. There's a wall and a stone with carving in it. It's a gravestone, you know, a headstone on which people write who is dead and what sort of person he or she was and dates and this kind of thing. I want you to copy out exactly what is on that stone. And I want you to do it without anyone knowing what you're about. Will you do that for me?"

"Sure. Just that?"

"Yes, just that."

He gave her directions which he insisted she write down. It was like a treasure hunt. He gave her the name of a street, Sailor's Lane. It was in Limehouse in the East End of London. He believed she would have to cross Tower Bridge, but she was a resourceful young lady and she could find the right bus. There was a chapel at the end of Sailor's Lane, opposite some wharfs. She was to go to the chapel and on its north exterior wall find the cornerstone that was shaped like a gravestone. The other stones that made the wall were rectangular. This was the stone. As she was writing she would be standing on the remains of a man, long-since dead.

She wrote down the directions and she looked up.

Why had he asked her to do it? Wasn't there anyone else he trusted?

Was it a game?

"How many devils were there when they made you play Faust?"

"In the play? There were six."

"And you saw seven and it struck you dumb?"

"I didn't say that."

"So you saw six?"

"No sir, I saw nine! OK?"

The old man nodded.

"Good, go and get this piece. A favor to a very old and foolish man."

The bus crossed Tower Bridge. Rose sat on the top deck and looked at the river on both sides. The miniature gray towers of a ship stuck out on the right and a police launch made its way past the Isle of Dogs to Greenwich Reach. The seat she sat in had come loose and she was conscious that the other passengers were looking at her as she adjusted herself on it, keeping her feet on the floor.

The place was difficult to find. The old man's memory of the area was either not reliable or the roads and buildings had changed. She looked at the rough map she had drawn. There were tourists walking along the cobbled streets which ran parallel to the river, with old wharfs converted into smart dwellings and offices on either side. No one could confuse her with the tourists — she was what she appeared to be, a London errand girl following rough-and-ready directions.

The place Mr. B had directed Rose to was a churchyard. It was now behind some land which was being built on. There were bulldozers and the preliminary marks of building work — breeze blocks and sand dunes where the land had already been cleared and stacks of timber under plastic sheets. An old iron fence surrounded the church which stood untouched in its plot of land, headstones of graves strewn randomly around it.

She found the stone straight away. It was engraved and the engraving had been worn down and was faint. The top of it was rounded like a headstone. She wasn't being observed so she approached the corner of the chapel. The words were not difficult to read close up. She noted them down. Eight lines of verse:

> The parting fancy of a player's speech
> Before the night on thrifty tones doth fall
> And each as witness turns an ear to each
> 'Fore darkness covers watchers, shades and all,
> Must to men's thoughts proclaim the intent whole
> That summed the bitter action of the play.
> So let confession be my last parole
> As night would speak to o'erweening day

The ground was wet where Rose crouched to copy down the verse. She looked around again to see if she was being observed. People were entitled to take notes in churchyards, weren't they? She'd spent half an hour just finding the wretched place. If the old man was so clever he should have been able to give her better directions. It occurred to her that the ability to give clear directions was a mark of smartness. Her mother always said ten yards when she meant a hundred, or turn left when she meant follow the road around a gentle bend.

Rose stood up. She read what she had copied. It didn't make much sense. He'd asked her to write the full stops, commas and all. Then it struck her that there wasn't a full stop. What did "parole" mean? Someone who comes out of jail for good behavior?

The last two lines didn't make sense by themselves. She bent down again and found that the mud at the base of the stone was easy to shift with the end of her pen. There was more writing below.

She looked for a sharp stone to use as a trowel and scratched at the mud which covered the stone. As she did it she looked over her shoulder. There were a couple of people passing through the graveyard but they didn't seem to notice her. Soon she could see the next line. Then another. Then another. She dug to a depth of a foot or more.

There were six more lines. She scraped them clean of earth.

Or light defines in opposition shade,
Wringing from departing night the dew,
With chill reminder even as I fade
That day and darkness duets will pursue
    And as eclipse doth mar the sun on high
    The low may yet the mighty's gain decry.

Mr. Bernier was probably a little crazy. What did he want all this stuff for? She counted the lines she had copied. Fourteen. She knew that was a sonnet. She read it again and some of it made sense. It was the same with texts she read for the first time for her A-level course. Rose looked around. Not a soul anywhere. Nevertheless, she shoved the mud back. She did the job roughly and moved away. The sky was gray and a chestnut vendor was selling small bags to tourists, even in summer. The tourists spoke German and didn't seem bothered by the price that the girl in sawn-off gloves charged them.

Rose got on a bus and went upstairs. She had the poem in

her pocket. A man in a checked jacket sat behind her. When she turned around she thought he was looking deliberately away from her, staring to the front of the bus. She thought she'd seen him somewhere before, buying chestnuts, placing flowers on one of the graves, watching her from beyond the wall. Maybe not. This sort of guy wasn't everywhere, but you could imagine him anywhere.

When she got off in Brixton he must have already got off because he wasn't behind her or anywhere on the bottom deck. Or she had imagined such a person.

Mr. B was waiting for her.

Rose handed him the sheet of paper. He pulled out another sheet of paper and gave it to her. It had a verse on it, written in an elaborate hand.

Her eyes went down the paper. It was the same sonnet she had just copied out. He'd sent her for nothing. He had a copy all the time.

"You'd copied it before?"

He read her trend of thought.

"No, no, no. I needed this. I worked it out. Where it would be. Believe me. This is from a different source. It's like a . . . a discovery."

He went to the drinks cabinet and pulled out two glasses and some sherry. He poured them and to Rose's amazement offered her one. "It's great to be right," he said, "but look carefully. I'm not a hundred per cent right."

Rose sipped the sherry. She wasn't used to it. She'd go down to the pub with her schoolmates or sometimes with the boys and girls from the estate, but they never drank sherry.

"The last lines," he said.

She read to the end of the sonnet, her eyes skimming the first twelve lines. It wasn't the same sonnet. The last two lines were different:

> The Promise of the gems that under lie
> Tho' shedding light shall only shades descry.

"We have them on the run, girl."

He banged the sheet of paper twice.

"It's here. Don't you see it? Daylight through an open window in the tropics."

He reached out for the copy he'd given her.

"I can see they are different," Rose said.

"Tch, tch, child. Wait a minute. Just wait a minute. You know those puzzles that you children are given. Find out how these two pictures are different, that sort of thing. Then they say find the hidden words in this sentence. You play those games, don't you?"

"When I was a kid."

"Play it again, Sam."

"It's Rose."

"No. It's an expression."

He thrust the lines she had copied in front of her. "Don't you see it?"

"I don't know what you mean."

"What was the name of your demon playwright?"

She read the lines at which he was pointing:

> And as eclipse doth mar the sun on high
> The low may yet the mighty's gain decry.

25

"The lines were covered up," she said. "I had to dig."

"You did well."

Then she saw it. Mar — Low.

"That's not how it's spelt. It has an 'e,' " Rose said.

"They didn't care about spelling. They used to call him Marley like your ballad singer, the black feller from Jamaica, or just M–A–R–I–O. Anything. But there it is."

"So Christopher Marlowe is buried there?"

He looked at her.

"Child, if you start saying these things, they'll carry you away to the lunatic asylum."

"We don't call it that anymore. It's mental hospital or the psychiatric wing."

"Yes, that's where they'll send you if you start telling them you know a man who has these sonnets spinning around in his head or you've found the long-lost burial place of the real Marlowe."

For the first time she saw it, a steely threatening quality under his kindness. He was saying to her that they were in this together, that she couldn't betray his trust. If she told anyone, well, she ran the risk of looking silly. All her life Rose had attempted to reassure herself that she wasn't standing out from the crowd, duller, slower, uglier, or even quicker, faster, more beautiful. And she'd learnt that being black she could be, just about, any of these things. But not ridiculous. She had seen her mother's black friends laugh amongst themselves and make fun of each other and it seemed okay there, but not in general society. The last thing to be was black and mad. There'd be no sympathy.

Rose gave her mother the money that Mr. B had given her.

Mom was worried. "Are you going to be all right living by yourself?"

She had the neighbors, Rose said.

"Mrs. Ullah has cleaned out their daughter's bedroom for me and I've moved my stuff in there and given them a key to our flat. We've sort of joined up the flats. I'll sleep in their house and eat there, but come and go from home."

Mr. and Mrs. Ullah had come to see Rose's mother and brought her some flowers and chocolate. They said they'd look after Rose.

The doctors said Mom had to have a serious operation on her stomach and would be in the hospital at least a month.

"So you want to be an actress?" Mr. B asked.

"When I get my results I'm going to university or drama school. They want two Bs for university. And for the drama schools, I've done interviews and auditions."

"And why do you want to be an actress? Don't you know that everyone who acts for a living has to be a fool?"

"Why?"

"Because they want to be someone else for the significant part of their lives. They want to be directed. The story is written by someone else. The emotions are supplied. The rest of us, we write our own stories, we fight for our own emotions."

"Actors and actresses have personal emotions too."

The old man laughed.

"Suppose your fairy godmother said, 'no acting, choose another career,' what would you choose?"

"Maybe writing. Journalism or television, I don't know. I've got ideas."

"The thing is not to have ideas, the thing is to write. If you want to be a writer, get a pen, typewriter. Get some paper. Write, for God's sake."

"It's not really as easy as that."

"It is."

"I read a lot for my exams and it never seemed easy, the plays and novels and poems."

"Tell me something, child. If your mother hadn't fallen ill, what would you be doing now? I mean, with your time before going to college?"

"I don't know. I'd applied for a creative writing course and I was going to go to a black theater group and work for them if they'd let me. But that's evenings. I'd have to work and earn some money."

"All right. This creative writing business. Suppose I tell you I used to be a writer and a teacher?"

"I believe that."

"Well, I'll teach you how to write. And maybe I'll put you off acting too. Lousy profession, man, just leave it alone."

Rose said she was willing to learn.

The old man nodded. He was not falling asleep, but he shut his eyes as though he were thanking God for an answered prayer.

Mr. B dictated in a crisp, high-pitched voice and Rose wrote frantically. He went into a sort of trance. He paced about the room. Every now and then he apologized for this method of work. The fingers on his right hand had to be exercised. As he dictated, he pulled them with the fingers of his left, bending, wriggling in a slow circular rhythm.

"Longhand, all the time longhand — but look at the longhand now."

"What's longhand?"

"Writing, man, ordinary writing. Beautifully formed letters. I had to do copy-book writing in . . . er . . . back home . . . when I was a schoolboy. And if you got a loop wrong you got a wallop. A smack."

If he ran on too fast and strong, Rose slowed him down, scribbling desperately.

He glanced over what she had written. It was as though he wasn't really interested in reading what he had dictated for accuracy or style or anything else. There was no vanity involved in forming the sentences, no satisfaction in something that was well said.

He never told her what task they were engaged on.

Of course Rose got to wondering who Mr. Bernier was. He wasn't Mr. Bernier, that was for sure. Her mother said she had seen his injured hand and wrist when he took the leather stirrup off it. She didn't know how he'd hurt himself.

There was always someone else in the house. Rose got to know the three men who looked after him and said they were gardeners or chauffeurs. One of them did fool around in the garden, pulling up weeds and using the hose, but why they said they were chauffeurs, she didn't know, because the old man didn't have a car and he never went out.

Rose came to the house at seven each morning and left at six in the evening in time to get home and then to the hospital. Once, when Mr. Bernier asked Rose to fetch a newspaper from the lounge on the ground floor, she found one of the men asleep in front of the television. His jacket lay open and he was snoring. Under his jacket there was a pistol in a holster. The holster was buttoned, not like the open ones in Westerns. The black butt of a revolver could be clearly seen.

Rose didn't ask Mr. B about that. She was getting used to this household, to his ways. She did what her mother had done for him — boiling eggs, cooking simple meals, shopping, running clothes through the washing machine and dryer and ironing them, vacuuming the carpets and, in between, all this typing for him.

He would leave her alone in the study with her notes and she would type them out.

The old man worked, dictated, read. Very occasionally he watched TV — cricket in the afternoons and sometimes, when he asked her to stay late, she saw that he watched opera when it came on in the evenings. He had a sound system which he called a gramophone, with CDs of Mozart and Beethoven.

Sometimes when Rose was typing in the study, she would hear the sound of heavy piano chords crashing like trays of crockery down the stairs. Modern stuff.

Rose was mostly alone with Mr. B.

He would read the newspapers avidly. He had the English papers, American papers, West Indian newspapers, and then he had an envelope which the Inspector brought each week with cuttings in it. The cuttings Rose was not allowed to see. Mr. B took them into his bedroom and put them in scrapbooks and drawers. Rose knew about them because her mother told her that he was a bit of a miser for cuttings. He kept them and guarded them as though they were gold.

Rose didn't follow the meaning of the writing as she took it down and retyped it. Her attention was on getting the words down, not on absorbing their meaning.

"Mr. Bernier, is this a story we're writing? I thought you said you'd tell me something about structure and all that."

"Of course it's a story, dear child, but the story hasn't begun. That's what we have to do, start at the beginning, then we get to the middle and then the end. That's the most difficult thing, to know what comes before what."

Rose studied the bookshelves. A set of Dickens, Henry James, D. H. Lawrence, and also shelves full of histories by writers she hadn't heard of. Black histories of Africa, the West Indies, the Caribbean. Books of all descriptions: poetry, novels, biography, and shelves and shelves full of books with figures and statistics in them. A small personal library.

When Mr. B had finished writing what he called a memoir, he sent her to get some champagne. He asked for three bottles. He opened one himself, he gave one to the Inspector and he asked Rose to take one to her mother. Rose got to the hospital early and drank the bottle of champagne with two of the nurses and a young doctor who said he'd risk a glass.

Leaving her mother each time was difficult. Mom had a tube stuck into her and a plastic bag by the side of the bed which filled up with yellow and red stuff in the slightly greenish water. Her mother looked as though her eyelids were a weight, a burden fixed to her brow.

Rose had made friends with the nurses and doctors. Each night when she walked out of the hospital, she felt something of the chill of being alone. She'd catch the bus home, or on a dry night she'd walk. The days were long and the roads were still light.

Her footsteps would echo as she walked down the empty hospital corridors and she'd be thinking and trying to force herself not to think about her mother being dead. Tok, tok, tok, tok, her footsteps would echo in the tiled corridors. She had assured Mom that the Ullahs were practically living in their flat. They were taking care of her. Then there was the old man.

Rose blocked out the thought each time it came to her, which was at least three or four times a day, the thought that her mother would die in the hospital and she'd have no one. She'd be alone. Except for the old man. Her mother had worked for him for years and she had kept his secret. No one on the estate knew exactly where Mom worked. Her friends knew that she worked as a sort of housekeeper for a rich family, but she had never told anyone about the old man. Now it seemed the old man trusted Rose with his secret too. If Mom died, the old man would help her. But then what would she do? Go to college? Try and look for her dad? In Africa? It was too terrifying to think about. Perhaps she should ask Mom for more clues as to where her dad might be, but she didn't want to do that because she knew that her mother would guess the reason for the question. She didn't want her to think that she, too, was thinking about her sudden death.

The old man took sleeping pills, very strong ones. He had other pills for ailments, real or imaginary, Rose didn't know.

"Your mother normally does this, child, but I suppose you'd better go. In this wretched country you have to get a doctor to write you a prescription for these pills. If it was the U.S., I could step out the door, go to a shop and drug myself silly if I wanted."

The old man gave her directions. Rose was to go to North London, to Finsbury Park. She was to see the receptionist at the doctor's office and register herself as a patient. Then when she was called in to see the doctor, she was to say that the old man wanted another prescription.

"Don't use my name. Just say 'the old man' sent you. The doctor will understand. There are two types of pills. One for sleep and one set for the clock. You may as well get those too."

"Are you sure he'll understand? I mean, I'll look a bit silly if he doesn't know what I'm talking about, won't I?"

"Trust me."

Rose found the address Mr. B had given her. An old three-story building on the main road, it was badly in need of paint and repair. Five steps led to the large door which was wedged open with a brick. An old metal plate declared that this was the practice of Dr. Trench.

Rose gathered her courage and went in. There were about a dozen people in the reception room awaiting their turn. She went to the window in the rickety partition and a young black man peered up at her from his register of cards.

"Name?"

"I'm not registered with the doctor yet."

"Do you want an appointment today, or are you just registering?"

"I'd like to see him today, please!"

"Her," the young man said, his eyes shining with mischief. "Both the doctors in this practice are women."

Both the doctors? The old man hadn't told her there were

two, or that they were women. Rose had assumed it was a man.

The young man thrust a form in front of her. "Can you fill this out, please, with your address and the number of your medical card and the name of your present physician."

Rose filled out the form and told the young man that she didn't know the number of her medical card but she was in severe pain and could she see the doctor anyway? She'd fetch her card from home that afternoon.

The young man asked her to take a seat.

Rose looked at the tattered magazines on the table in the center of the room. There were a couple of old Sunday color supplements and a stack of travel brochures for the Caribbean which were just as ragged. Rose picked one up. The other patients sat quietly.

There were two red bulbs on either side of the door leading to the offices from the reception room. Each time a patient was called, one or the other bulb would light up and the receptionist would call out the name of the next patient.

Rose was nervous now. Did the old man mean either doctor? He had given her instructions which sounded very much as though he didn't know there would be two doctors in this office. When Rose's turn came the man shouted her name.

"Rose Hassan, room two, please."

She walked down the dark corridor and knocked at the door on the right. A voice called her in and Rose found herself standing in a very bright, clean, pleasant room. A young woman sat in a chair at the desk and smiled at her.

"Rose Hassan? Come in, take a seat. Now what seems to be the matter?"

Rose was thinking that the matter was that she was in the

wrong place. This woman doctor was young, blonde, pretty.

Rose didn't sit down. "I haven't come for myself," she said.

"Oh."

"I've come for the old man," Rose blurted out. As soon as she'd said it, she knew it hadn't performed the magic that it should have.

"Which old man would that be?" asked the doctor. She was smiling, but obviously puzzled.

"It doesn't matter," said Rose, in a panic now, wondering whether she should turn and rush out. "But he did say he knew you or you would know . . ."

"I think I know what you are saying," said the doctor. "You probably want to see my colleague. Maybe she knows the old man."

"Yes. Please."

"Well, go out and tell Herbert then, Rose."

Rose didn't need the prompt. She was out of the door saying she was sorry.

She was blushing. She went to the receptionist.

"I wanted Dr. Trench," she said.

"I know," said the young man, grinning. "You see they are both called Dr. Trench. You mean Dr. A. Trench, not Dr. K. Trench. You can go next. Door to the left this time, Ms. Hassan."

The door to the left was a little further down the corridor and an old, strong but fluted voice said "Come in" when Rose knocked.

Yes, she'd come to the right place. Dr. A. Trench was a black woman with an American accent, probably sixty years old.

"I've come for the old man," Rose said, full of confidence now.

"I see. And where did he get you?"

"I work for him. My mother used to work for him, but she's ill."

"That would be Mrs. Hassan?"

Rose nodded.

"I'm very sorry to hear it. I expect the old man wants his doses."

Dr. Trench wrote out the prescriptions.

"Tell him it's okay, I'm not keeping a copy of them," Dr. Trench said.

Rose took the prescriptions.

"Is the old fox okay?"

"I think he's very well."

"What do you do for him?"

Rose didn't know whether she should answer this, but as she hesitated, Dr. Trench answered it for her.

"Another book, is it?"

Rose nodded.

"When he'll see me, he should send you over. I'll come out."

Dr. Trench shook Rose's hand.

Rose rushed out of the office to the Tube station.

She went to Mr. B's and he sent her out again to get the pills.

She didn't tell Mr. B about the two Dr. Trenches, one young and white, the other old and black, and about her mistake.

That evening she went to the hospital and then home.

36

The next day the old man dictated all morning and Rose spent the rest of the day typing it all up.

She got home late. She had the keys to both flats, their own and the Ullahs and she was carrying Mom's laundry from the hospital. She thought she'd leave it in their flat before she went to the Ullahs' to sleep.

She turned the key and entered their flat. It felt funny.

Rose looked through the two bedrooms and the kitchen. She went into the bathroom. When she went into her own room, her desk, her books, she was sure they'd been examined. She looked through her pile of files on the shelf, at the notebooks. Someone had thumbed through them. No. That was ridiculous. She couldn't actually remember which book or piece of paper was where, but she felt they weren't quite at the angle she had left them.

Nothing was missing. If someone had been there, they left no sign as to how they had gotten in. But then the front door had only an ordinary lock and even Rose had seen boys from her primary school, let alone professional thieves, opening up doors with pins and pieces of wire and filed-off master keys.

If nothing had been taken, why did they come, Rose asked herself. Maybe if they hadn't taken anything, they brought something! She didn't say anything to the Ullahs. They were all asleep by the time she went next door. She would tell them the next morning. Mr. Ullah would call the police, but the police never solved any crimes on their estate, though they came around and were fairly active in the area, strutting around and taking some of the boys in.

One day Mr. B stopped dictating. He'd come to the end of the first part of a story and he turned to Rose and said,

"Do you know something about your school's foundation?"

"It was named after the three martyrs, that's all I know — and a bit about why they were killed, the religious factions and secret societies with Catholics defying Henry VIII, all that. Born again as a true anti-pope opportunist and history's most famous sexist pig. I find his wives more interesting."

"Do you know it began as a 'hospital' for young men?"

"No."

"May I tell you something about this great and good institution of learning of which you are an alumnus?"

"How do you know about it?"

"These stupid things are what old age is made of. How long it takes a caterpillar to crawl from Cairo to the Cape. Useless knowledge. All mine. And your school. The Martyrs. You know your school was started by an actor?"

Rose said she did.

"Hmm. A friend of Christopher Marlowe, who years after Marlowe's death began to see devils on stage. He believed that his brain had turned feverish, that the creatures weren't actually there even if he saw them. He knew that his friend Marlowe had been an atheist and the member of a circle that discussed the world without God or religion. These are his actual words: 'I count religion but a childish toy / And hold there is no sin but ignorance.'

"They even began to discuss the beginnings of modern science, mixed up with witchcraft and 'skills' and crafts of all sorts for which they sought explanations. He started the school as a sort of safe bet. If there was a God, well he had started a school for clever boys and done some good on earth. If there was no supernatural, then he was a great revolutionary hero for starting a school which had the express intent of being scientific and not religious."

"How do you know all this? I mean, is it in a book?"

"Again, I want you to do something for me. Can you get into school during the holidays?"

"There's conferences and things there. Everyone's gone."

"Everyone? Even the people who look after the buildings?"

"Mr. Rafferty? He'll be there. He has to run the conferences and keep the place clean or whatever."

"Friend of yours?"

"Sort of. He's black and we recognize each other."

"Good. Take a camera, go into the chapel and take photographs of the three stained-glass windows. Do you know how to take photographs?"

Mr. B produced an expensive-looking camera.

"It's good and doesn't give trouble. You've got to look through the thing and press the button."

"Yes, sure. We did photography at school. What do you take me for?"

"I do apologize," said Mr. B. "I can never figure these damn things out, man. If they were guns, I would have shot myself."

Rose made her way to school. Mr. Rafferty was there as she had thought. The chapel stood a little aloof from the imposing red school buildings and the new block which was concrete with imitation Gothic windows.

There was no point in telling Mr. Rafferty any lies.

"I'd like to take pictures of the place, Mr. Rafferty, just to keep, you know, because I've only got pictures of the other kids and some of the teachers."

"Some of the teachers," said Mr. Rafferty. He had a habit of repeating your last words.

"I mean I want some of the school, the buildings."

"The buildings," said Mr. Rafferty.

"Just to keep, put on the walls in my room at university."

"Room at university," said Mr. Rafferty. He began to cackle. His laugh was contagious. Rose always thought that he had a natural kindness in his eyes.

He opened the chapel for her and she took her photographs. He was king of the buildings and he felt flattered that someone wanted to take pictures of them. Especially the only black girl in the class.

When the twenty-four or so colored prints were developed and enlarged, they were quite beautiful to look at.

Mr. B began to point things out. He knit his brows. He told Rose, "Look at the pictures at the top of each of the windows. Anything?"

"The glass looks a bit distorted."

"Precisely, dear girl. They are older, the original pictures. Other pictures lower down have been replaced. We'll never know if they were reproductions of the old pictures, but the top ones are untouched. Look at the first one, Christ on the cross and two desciples. Notice anything again?"

"I saw that when I was taking the pictures. They're kneeling on either side and one is black and the other white."

"And the Christ figure?"

"That's funny because He's holding His own cross. Or it's a thunderbolt or something to strike down the wicked."

"Or it could be a spear?"

"What would He be doing with a spear?"

"Doesn't matter. And His face?"

"I thought the glass had run and blanked out the features, it's plain."

40

"It was always plain. It never had features. Or so I believe."

"And there's some writing. It says, 'What we behold is censured by our eyes.' "

"You are doing excellently. And the next window, this, a picture within a picture. A cross, a stained glass picture within a stained glass picture and an empty tomb hovering under it."

"Christ escapes or is reborn?"

"No, I think the man who made the windows was instructed somewhat differently. Empty tomb, yes. Christ? Christopher? Maybe. Then the third one."

"A sea and a hand with a cross emerging from it. The story of King Arthur or something?"

"No, again a hint, note the color of the arm thrust above the sea and something else you've missed."

"I didn't miss it, I thought it was a convention. The sun has a face."

"But what about the face?"

"Angel white boy stereotype, blue eyes, golden hair . . ."

Mr. B said, "I'm nearly sure now."

"Of what?"

"It's a pity you can't dig up the floor of your school chapel. And dear child, look carefully again. That's not a cross, is it?"

"It's a bit like an arrow."

"Perhaps it's a spear held in this black hand."

More poetry the next day.

By the time Rose got there the old man had scribbled something out in his shaky creepy-crawly hand.

"I copied this out because I didn't want to spring the

damn thing on you. But read it and tell me what you think about it."

Rose took the sheet of paper and tried reading it.

"No, aloud, man, aloud."

So she read it aloud:

"A woman's face with nature's own hand painted
    Has thou, the master-mistress of my passion;
    A woman's gentle heart, but not acquainted
    With shifting change, as is false women's fashion;
    An eye more bright than theirs, less false in rolling,
    Gilding the object whereupon it gazeth;
    A man in hue, all 'hues' in his controlling,
    Which steals men's eyes and women's souls amazeth.
    And for a woman wert thou first created;
    Till nature, as she wrought thee, fell a-doting,
    And by addition me of thee defeated,
    By adding one thing to my purpose nothing.
    But since she prick'd thee out for women's pleasure,
    Mine be thy love, and thy love's use their
    treasure."

"Now tell me what that is."

"It's a poem. A sonnet."

"Good. And who wrote it for whom?"

"I don't know."

"But their sex is pretty obvious, isn't it?"

Rose looked again at the poem.

"It's from one man to another. He loves him. They're probably gay or something."

"Brilliant. Just what I thought. And this thing about 'hue,' what's all that?"

"It sounds like the man to whom he's writing is a man of some color. He could be black, and because he controls 'hues' or colors or something, I suppose he's a painter."

"Those fellers thought writing was also full of colors. He could be a writer."

"All right then, a writer."

Mr. B picked up a paperback book from the coffee table. He had put torn bits of paper in it as page markers. He handed it to Rose and asked her to turn to the first marker.

She looked at the book. William Shakespeare. *The Sonnets*. Number 20. It was the same poem.

"Turn to Number 147."

Rose did.

"Read the last few lines."

Rose read the lines:

> "For I have sworn thee fair and thought thee bright
> Who art as black as hell, as dark as night."

"Another love poem to a black person," said Mr. B.

"Love poem? The way he puts it is not very nice, is it? I mean if a boyfriend or someone said that to me, I wouldn't be flattered."

"Maybe," said Mr. B. "I suspect that by the time he is writing Numbers 146 and 147, he's fed up with the person or he's fed up with the hypocrisy of not saying it. This person was black, what was the world going to do about it?"

"Shakespeare loved a black woman?" asked Rose.

"I don't know who Shakespeare loved at all."

"John Murray," said Mr. B, "was a publisher who did risky things. He published Byron, a risky writer in his time."

"Like a video nasty man?" asked Rose.

"No, no, no. Video nasties are risky because they are just nasty. This feller specialized in bold gestures." Mr. B was contemplative. "I suppose you should copy the manuscript before taking it out of the house. That'll be your next job."

"What manuscript? Why don't I photocopy it down at the library, or wait till school starts and use the English department machine?"

"Won't do. I can't let this thing out of my sight. It was lost once before. It came into the hands of Murray who mentions it in some letters to Byron and to other friends.

"It was dynamite, this stuff. Murray wasn't sure whether it was real at all or some sort of forgery. In the late eighteenth and early nineteenth century there was a lot of nonsense about black magic and the like going on. Murray had an employee who was into all this stuff and he copied the whole book. Which was just as well because Murray's place caught fire and everything was destroyed.

"Murray writes to his friends saying that this is a great loss to history but he never says why. Now I have the copy made by this feller who, of course, kept it secret from Murray and tried to sell it himself."

"What is it?" Rose asked, looking at the manuscript in a leather folder.

"The story starts a few centuries before John Murray and Byron and the fire and this employee. These are the diaries of one Simon Forman. A feller who lived in Elizabethan times. We know a lot about him, because he was a scientist and a magician and necromancer and all sorts of other things, suspicious things. We know of him because he went to plays in his own time and copied out what was said on stage, word for word, and preserved the manuscripts. We have his version of several Shakespeare plays and Marlowe and Kyd and other playwrights. He was a bit suspect, robbing graves and mixing with very shady characters. He ended up in prison several times for his beliefs. I believe this is the diary he left, which of course he couldn't publish while he was alive because the stuff in it is quite incredible.

"Thank God for the thief, man. Okay, that's the story, now let me tell you something."

"What sort of thing?" asked Rose.

"I don't want you talking about this manuscript or taking any pages of it out of here."

"I won't."

"I don't suppose it really matters. If you do people will think you're crazy."

The Diary Of Simon Forman (1552–1611)

AS IT PERTAINS TO LAZARUS THE SLAVE AND TO
SEVERAL DISCOVERIES AMONG MEN AND THEIR
FATES.

FEBRUARY 12TH, 1592

I go as spectator to the court when in public is held the trial of
seven men who are likely to hang. They are charged with mutiny and piracy. Tales of their doings are spreading through
Southwark and the city and one may go to any place of gathering, an ale house, a theater and hear reports and rumors of
their roguery.

The mob is a collection of cut-purses and villains such as
should be themselves hanged. It is these citizens of London
who love a hanging and hang on the words of accusers and
judges. I note two who stand together and cross themselves
every time death and killing is mentioned. I know these
rogues have themselves taken payment for murder. They
gather in the courts day after day to feel more at liberty than
less fortunate rogues. Thankful perhaps that they stand a little removed from the shadow of the gallows which falls on
these seamen.

The black man who stands in the dock, speaks English like a Wiltshireman. He makes no gesture when his fellow pirates accuse him of dealing with the Devil and tell stories of his gruesome feats and of his devilish powers.

The black man is named Henry and the master of the ship whom he has murdered was called Walsh. So our blackamoor is charged in the name of Walsh's Henry.

My Lord Protector of London who tries the case and is known to treat prisoners with the ceremony that befits gentlemen, but is known also to hang them with the contempt reserved for rats, calls him "Mr. W.H." From my Lord Proctor's way of turning the words in his mouth, I know that these wretches will surely hang and be buried in unconsecrated ground. It is the talk of London. The theaters will be empty the day they mount these on the scaffold and thousands will attend to watch the gibbet crack their unfortunate necks.

I am visited by a thin, nervous man who would have me find facts and fates for him. He comes in secrecy and asks me to say nothing of his visit to any person.

"I come to you in desperation, Master Forman."

"Believe me, sir, you are no exception. Most men and many women who come to me come for no other reason."

"But mine is a passion I can bear no longer."

"And the lady does not return your love?"

He was taken aback. I had come to the root of the matter without his saying what it was that perturbed him.

"Perhaps she feels she is of higher station than yourself and will not lower herself in the estimation of the world."

A sigh escaped the thin man. His moustache on a narrow and bony face looked like a huge yoke placed on a feeble ox.

"It is, alas, worse! I am a gentleman and man of means and position. The woman in question is no lady. A strumpet sir, a woman of the streets. And yet she shuns me."

"And where did you meet her?"

"Sir, I met her in a professional way."

"You paid her and now she demands more and more."

"No, no, no, Master Forman, I have paid her nothing for her favors. I have never been granted these favors. The profession I speak of was mine, not hers."

"Ah, I see," I said, not seeing much in reality.

"I met her, this angel in devil's guise, Lilly she is called, when she was restrained and brought to my care. I, sir, am the warden of Marshalsea prison hard by here and being suspected of theft she was given over to the care of the prison."

The warden coughed. A sign that he would make a confession if I could keep his secret.

"Master Forman, it is often that we who are entrusted with the care of these miscreants, thieves, harlots, murderers, cut-purses, pirates, vermin of every description . . . it is often that we in Christian charity speak to them and ask them to repent their sins and we talk to them of their lives and misdeeds."

"Yes, I have heard from my acquaintance that you ask these thieves to give you some of their money. As part of their repentance, of course."

"Master Forman, you are a man of great wisdom as I was told, and you understand me well."

"I also believe that of the women who are delivered to your prison, other little tokens of Christian repentance and love are demanded?"

"Master Forman, I can swear I never laid a finger on Lilly

48

Camby. She did me no favor, though I begged her and I released her when she gave me hope that I could visit her when she was a free woman."

"So you released Mistress Camby and then pursued her?"

The warden looked abashed but was determined now to tell me what was in his his heart.

"Such a devil has never possessed me, sir. You must help. She is unbending. She spurns me. Why, yesterday I called at the tapster's house where she has employment and she declared to all the company that I was a jack and slave who lived off the fortune of his wife and from the earnings of thieves from whom I took commissions."

"And do you?"

To this Master Warden made no reply. He looked straight at me. "I wish to be released from the pain of wanting the creature. Some physic, some spell can surely bring quiet to my heart. I think of nothing else, sir. I believe she has bewitched me. She mocks me. She makes me a laughing-stock. She accepts all my gifts and refuses my protestations. She sent the letters I wrote her to my wife."

"Master Warden, it is a common case, a common malady. I have some answers. But first tell me. You mentioned in your list of evil-doers in your care, the pirates."

"Indeed, I did, sir."

"May I then ask if a certain blackamoor by the name of Mr. W.H. has been presented to your prison?"

"Yes, sir, he has. He is there and awaits the decision of the Privy Council which will confirm for the Queen the sentence of hanging upon him and upon those others as were with him and took the lives of the Christian officers of their ship."

"Sir, I wish to speak to him. I may learn something from

him of the arts of Africa which will be useful in your case. We shall relieve you of the pain of your longing and we shall do it by casting a spell on your Lilly Camby, who may perchance immediately begin to be your slave in affection and deed."

The warden's uneven teeth broke into a smile under the moustache.

LATE ONE NIGHT, in fact it must have been the early
hours of the morning, Mr. B got up and went to the
bathroom. His legs felt weak. He fell and smashed his head
on the edge of the bathtub.

The next morning Rose was late. She had told Mr. B that
she needed to go to the stationers before she came in that day
and she didn't get to Mr. B's till ten-thirty.

The Inspector was there and he greeted Rose very cheerily.
"I haven't heard the old man stirring. Sleeping like a baby, I
think."

Rose found the old man, his head in a pool of blood,
breathing hard. It looked strange, the dried blood on his
white hair. She didn't panic or shout. She tried to lift him and
then went downstairs and summoned the Inspector, who
rushed up the stairs. Together they managed to drag him to
the carpet of the bedroom and put him down.

The Inspector said, "Now that's a pickle. The old horse
won't have a doctor. If we save him, he'll be furious when he
recovers."

"There is one doctor who knows him," Rose said.

"There's nothing for it, but to get him fixed up. I hope it
hasn't affected his memory. A very expensive memory, that
one," said the Inspector.

Rose looked up the phone number of Dr. Trench. She rang it. The phone was answered by the young black receptionist, Herbert.

"Dr. Angelina Trench won't come out on any calls. You can have Dr. Kate Trench."

"That won't do, it has to be Dr. Angelina," said Rose.

"Well, I'm not going to be the one to break the news. What was your name again?"

"My name is Rose Hassan, but you'll have to tell her I'm calling because the old man has knocked himself out."

There was a long silence.

"Just hold on. Can you give me the address?" said the young man.

Rose cupped her hand over the phone.

She spoke to the Inspector.

"The address please," the receptionist said at the other end, "Dr. Angelina will come out."

"He wants the address!"

The Inspector shook his head.

"Tell them you'll pick the doctor up from a Tube station because it's difficult to find."

Rose told Herbert just that.

"Please tell the doctor it's urgent. He's knocked himself out."

"Try smelling salts. The doctor will be with you as soon as possible." The voice sounded urgent, excited even.

It took an hour for the doctor to arrive. Rose picked her up from the Tube station in a minicab.

Dr. Trench carried a black bag. When they got to the house she dashed in.

"Where is he?"

As Rose shut the door behind them she thought a car had passed the gate, up the road and then down it again. It seemed to be going slowly and Rose had the distinct sensation that someone in the car was driving past to look into the house. She forgot about it as she rushed upstairs, her heart thumping now for the first time with anxiety for the old man.

The doctor said Mr. B had had a nasty gash but there wasn't any need to be worried. She gave the old man some smelling salts and revived him. She told them he wasn't to be given any food or drink, especially not alcohol.

Mr. B was only faintly conscious, but he couldn't resist a remark. "Oh, God. It's you, you cruel old crocodile. How you mean no alcohol? How will a man survive?"

When Rose got home that evening and unlocked the door of the flat she looked over the balcony. The same car that she had seen passing Mr. B's house was parked in the courtyard of the estate. She went into the flat. She got her clothes and picked up Mom's clothes and put them in a bag. There were some letters for Mom which she stuffed in the bag.

She set off for the hospital.

The car was still there, a dark blue BMW. A young man was sitting inside it reading a newspaper. The car had a huge aerial suggesting that it was a minicab. The man stepped out as Rose came down the stairs. It was Herbert, the receptionist from Dr. Trench's office.

"Rose, can I have a word with you?" he asked. "I don't mean to startle you, and I'm not going to ask you if you want a lift or anything. Just one simple question. I am very concerned about . . . er . . . Mr. . . . Johnson's health."

"I don't know what you're talking about."

"I am his nephew, though you mustn't tell him I spoke to

53

you. He may be known to you by a different name. The gentleman you and your mother look after."

"Just leave me alone, I don't know what you're talking about."

"You see, it's because of him that I got the job with Dr. Trench. He was the one who introduced me to her. I don't want to extract any information involuntarily from you. I'm a relative and I'm just very concerned. I couldn't leave the office, you see. How serious is it? What's wrong with him?"

He was now walking alongside Rose.

"Why don't you ask the doctor?"

The young man didn't reply.

Then he said, "Look Rose, I'll leave you alone. I'm going now. Please, don't worry him by saying anything about me. One day, if you give me a chance I'll explain."

He stopped.

Rose suspected that there was something strange about this young man. She was even a little afraid of him. He didn't seem the sort of person who would be a doctor's receptionist at all. Maybe he was telling the truth. He turned and got into the car. No, it couldn't be a minicab, because he was driving it himself.

From The Diary Of Simon Forman

MARCH 4TH

I have seen Master Warden of Marshalsea and the next morning I go to the prison. I am admitted and led by himself to the
cell in which the black man, W.H., is kept.

I had heard very little of his speech when he was brought in
chains before his accusers from whom he is now separated.
One of them has, by confession and by accusing W.H. been
granted his own life and will not hang. The others, pirates
and murderers all, are condemned with the moor and await
the Queen's pleasure. They are all to be hung.

I greet the black man and make myself known to him.

Master Warden tells him that I am a Doctor of Arts and
wish to speak with him. The man is most gracious. What
business can he have with a Doctor of Arts who has not solved
the mystery of how to keep a man from the gallows? He
smiled a wan smile. Why should he speak?

"I came to the trials and, watching your accusers, I felt
they were all liars to a man."

Again W.H. says nothing, He is sitting on the pile of straw
and blanket which is his bed.

"So will you speak with the doctor?" says Master Warden. Finally the blackamoor speaks.

"I had thought you had come to accuse me further. Tell me doctor, do you know of a way to cheat the gallows?"

"No, I know of no such. I can offer you nothing."

"You mistake. You can offer me your company."

"Gladly, sir. In exchange I would know your story."

Thus he did agree to tell me what he did.

The warden would leave us and for several days after, I spoke to W.H. every day and noted what he had said. Here follows his story.

I estimate that at the time of telling this black man is approximately twenty-six years of age. I tell age by the depth of impression of lines on the hand and by looking at the teeth and the jaws. There is a science to it which is part of physic. Yet ignorance is king in our land and I was imprisoned years ago in Salisbury for what was called before my Lord Bishop an act of wizardly knowledge through witchcraft. I tell the story he told to me.

THE PLAIN TALE OF HENRY THE SLAVE FREED BY THE GRACE OF GOD AND A MIRACLE PERFORMED BY DOCTOR FORMAN, OF HIS TRAVEL ABROAD AND THE CAREER IN WHICH HE FINDS FAVOR IN LONDON.

For the first years of his life he had cut cane. From the time he was a child, through an early boyhood. On the plantation in Hispaniola they did not beat children. When the whiplash fell on your back, you knew you were a man. The others watched as the lashes fell and depending on the spirit you displayed, they would invite you to learn in secret the language of the ancestors. The slaves were given a ration of rum and they spoke amongst themselves of freedom. Though here, the end of the world, there was never any hope save that a miracle might happen and the God of these very Spaniards or the ghosts of the ancestors might come to set you free and carry you into the clouds.

The Portuguese priests had come to the island. The young man didn't understand why, but they had gathered many slaves together and preached to them about the father in Rome who would look after them and told them of the faithlessness of their masters. In Jesus would they find their freedom.

The island was a prison. He had seen the ships being loaded and unloaded. It was very rarely that human cargo came on the ships; new black men from the land they called home, starved, full of boils, diseased, chained, brought to the Gulf and auctioned in the market. Then the ships were restocked and the vats of dried cane juice and the raw rum in barrels would be loaded on. Now and then a story would reach their settlement, their gathering of huts, of black men who in defiance had gone to the hills and fought with their teeth and with staves and their bare hands and had been brought back to be publicly hanged or flogged in the plantation's squares. The stories didn't bother him. They were stories of other men and passions beyond those that moved him.

One day Father Da Silva told him, him alone, that he could run. But he must be baptized first. He came out in the light of the early morning sun to the appointed spot. There were twenty or thirty other slaves there and Da Silva went through the motion and ceremony of baptizing them. He told the small gathering that the ship they could see was waiting for them. It would take them to England. There were many wicked men there who did not believe in the true gospel of Jesus Christ, but the men on board *The Resurrection* were devoted to the duty of shepherding them to a new life.

There was no time to ask questions. The men from the supervisory crew, men from different plantations came with their muskets and just as he was kneeling to receive Father Da Silva's converting hand to his forehead, they began to shoot and everyone scattered.

The musket shot barked out just as the priest was about to anoint him, so in a flash, he took his baptism from the surf. He threw himself on to the waves and swam for all he was worth. The men came out of the savannah, the bushes, shooting their muskets as they came. The priest stood immobile, the shot flying around him but the young man, having received his name, was reborn and he swam like a devil to the waiting ship. A new name, for a new life. The priest shouted to him that he was to be called Lazarus.

She was a merchant ship with two masts flying the English flag. Her crew was on deck watching the strange scene on shore. Lazarus had no time to see if the others had followed him. As he swam with strong and steady strokes he fancied, the waves thundering in his ears, that he could hear the futile beat of arms swimming next to him, to the left and to the right. The water, he thought, was alive with black slaves swimming towards *The Resurrection*. Perhaps towards freedom.

Lazarus climbed the rope the seamen threw to him even as *The Resurrection* began to sail. He remembered being thrashed against the wood of the hull and the last fingers of water still clutching to reclaim him as he twisted on the rope, his hands bleeding, trying to get his feet square on the timbers and the faces of the seamen as they hauled him, scraping his half-naked body on to the deck. There he knelt and prayed with the matter of the ship, Mr. Walsh, who said, "Praise be to our Lord. Hail Mary, mother of God, that hath brought deliverance."

They dressed the black man in sailor's trousers and blue tunic and when they sailed north over many months, they gave him blankets and woolen garments and a cap which covered his head and ears and buttoned under his chin.

It was thus that Lazarus started learning English. Mr. Walsh, the master of the ship, was no teacher. He did not start with a lined page and the sound of the alphabet. He began reading to him translations of Greek and Latin poetry, of the histories of the ancient world, of plays. He would read to Lazarus while pacing about his board room, the black man staring at him, following his gesticulations with his eyes, understanding nothing at first.

"The text and patience," Mr. Walsh would say. He held the conviction, as did many men of enlightenment, that all God's creatures were infinitely educable, that anyone could be taught anything that another human being had mastered in mind.

For a year or more Lazarus did not know of what he spoke. He would go on deck with Mr. Walsh and he understood much better the instructions or the encouragement or blandishment that Mr. Walsh handed out to the crew or to Mr. Summers, the first mate. He began to understand the terms which the sailors used and the oaths which they swore. Mr. Walsh and Mr. Summers were the only ones on board who spoke Spanish and they treated Lazarus as a guest on board.

The rest of the crew, as far as Lazarus could make out, treated him sometimes as a companion traveler, sometimes as a piece of necessary cargo. You never need to know the language of men to know what attitude they take towards you.

Yet Lazarus was thirsty for knowledge. In the Spanish he spoke, he explained to Mr. Walsh that although he had a name at birth, he was called Lazarus by the priests. His own name was, even to him, lost for ever. Mr. Walsh read him, over and over again, the story of Lazarus from the Bible. Lazarus said he was not sure he should have been named after a dead man. His people worshipped their ancestors and when a person was dead he or she had moved on to a better place.

"A better place? Is my ship not good enough for you?" Mr. Walsh asked. "But we can change your name, of course. We shall call you Henry and Harry after our own kings."

So Lazarus came to be called Henry and he spent the nights on the ship learning to write by candlelight. The master had a history of the Greek wars which fascinated Henry and he heard over and over again the story of the Wars of the Ros.

The Resurrection unloaded its cargo of rum and sugar in France and an argument broke out between Mr. Summers and Mr. Walsh as to whether his ship, chartered as it was by a Portuguese company, should return to Portugal or make its way to the port of London whence they could pick up a new crew and could themselves return for a while to their homeland. Henry observed them poring over letters and newspapers. Finally the decision was taken to turn to Portugal, as was their duty and part of their contract. *The Resurrection* sailed to Cadiz.

The crew was displeased and showed their displeasure to the master and to Mr. Summers. Henry witnessed a meeting on deck with all the crew, in which arguments and disputation broke out. Mr. Summers addressed the crew on behalf of Mr. Walsh and conveyed to them their decision and their orders. The rum ration was increased and several promises of wealth to come were made. Then they were exhorted by Mr. Summers to get to their knees and pray. He had to shout to get them to their knees. The men stood square and silent and were reluctant to join in prayer till Mr. Walsh got to his feet. He glanced at Henry and there was an instruction in the glance. They all prayed together as dark gray clouds gathered over the Bay of Biscay and rain began to whip the deck of the ship.

From The Diary of Simon Forman

Each day I attend W.H. at the prison and though he protests that he knows no black arts, he tells me that he has possession of considerable learning from his travels and this intelligence he will give me. Master Warden awaits my calls at the Marshalsea prison. He is a man who lives in terror. Yesterday he had a patch about his eye where his wife had boxed him. I have given him charms to wear in the presence of his beloved Mistress Lilly Camby and he ties them on his arm as I have instructed. It keeps him from making enquiry and he seems to trust the charm.

"Master Forman, she smiled at me yesterday. It must be working."

W.H. is very anxious now to tell me his full story. I believe that he is completely innocent of the blood of Mr. Walsh and Mr. Summers. He says he loved both of them deeply and though he had no option now but to face the gallows, he wants it known by at least one person whom he trusts that he is innocent of all acts of piracy and that he was of the defending party when the sailors turned to mutiny and piracy. They would have killed him, too, but they were afraid of any powers he might have when he turned ghost, because he had terrified the mutineers by shouting curses in the African tongue he had been taught as a boy by the elder slaves in Hispaniola.

This is the tale he told as I have taken it down.

The Resurrection was contracted in Portugal, in Cadiz by a factor to pick up horses in Arabia and take them to the Indies. Thence we sailed.

We stopped at the port of Basra, a city of the Arabians, and the vessel was visited by many merchants who bargained with Mr. Summers in the language of the Turks. It is a city of great trade and merchandise, where dates and rice and corn are plentiful. To our hold were brought two hundred horses by diverse merchants. Mr. Walsh and Mr. Summers knew nothing of the care of animals. I myself, who in Hispaniola was entrusted with the horses and the oxen which pulled the machines grinding the cane, was much valued for the knowledge I conveyed to Mr. Walsh of the upkeep of the beasts.

We sailed with this cargo and every day we brought ponies on deck, where several of the crew, who were not in favor of the task we undertook, would take sport with them, mounting the ponies and riding them a few steps.

Thus we came to the Portuguese port of Goa in the Indies. It is the principal city, where the Portuguese have dominion and bring to the ships which lade there the spices and cloths and coin of the interior. Our Sovereign Majesty has no splendor to compare with the way these Portuguese in the Indies disport themselves. Our own mission was welcomed and the horses unloaded. They were to be taken over land, herded to the great kingdom of Bizaynagar which lies on the border beyond the villages and land which the King of Portugal may call his own Indies.

In the company of three Arabian merchants and two of our crew and Mr. Summers, we made the eight day journey to Bizaynagar, herding the two hundred horses before us. We resided there a full two months in which time I saw many strange things. The natives of that kingdom are Hindoos and do burn the corpses of the dead as they do not believe that God sent a son who will resurrect men in soul and body in the kingdom to come. Their womenfolk, being married to a man who dies, are required to cast themselves on the fire that burns his body and so perish with him.

The King of Bizaynagar, having taken the horses to his stable, turned us from his door and would not see us or our representations. No gold did he pay us nor thanks but turned us away as common beggars in the company of soldiers. We had come with expectations of great riches and returned now to Goa empty-handed.

We were the ruination of the crew and our prospects. We had come to the Indies with horses and departed with nothing but debt.

Mr. Walsh prayed for two nights and then decided that no help was to come from the Viceroy of the Portuguese and that his only recourse was to sail away penniless.

So low were we brought by the trick of the natives of the

Indies that we had no money to get rations for the ship for our journey back. Mr. Walsh had to borrow the gold from Portuguese spice merchants who, in all wonder, took nothing but the bare signatures of Mr. Walsh on trust, with a promise to pay them back once he reached Cadiz.

Three days into our voyage the malcontents of the crew, all of whom had been promised fortunes, turned against us. They arrested Mr. Walsh, Mr. Summers and myself who was their companion. Mr. Walsh entreated them to see the error they made. It was mutiny on the high seas and all they could hope for was a rope at the end of it. He was willing to forget that they had made bold but the men were stubborn in their resolve. They bound us between decks and took charge of the ship. We knew not from day to day whence we were sailing but on the thirtieth day we heard the guns of *The Resurrection* and witnessed preparation, with the men running to and fro from the deck to the gunwales and down below.

The men, as we guessed, had turned to piracy and looted several schooners, gathering many chests of merchandise and gold. They put people to their death and drank through the night, singing, cursing and fighting each other like savages.

Mr. Walsh would pray in prison and he kept our spirits up with stories and some reading from the books we were allowed. When the mutineers came down Mr. Summers at first threatened them and promised to say nothing of their mutiny if we were released and matters were restored to what they should be. The mutineers did not trust his word.

I for my part growled at them the curses we slaves had used on the slave drivers. This way they were terrified of me. It was a game and when the jailers had turned their backs, Mr. Walsh, Mr. Summers and I would laugh. Yet it was the game that perhaps saved my life.

Three of the crew fell mysteriously ill and their stomachs swole up and they were cursed with cramps. One of them died. It was a fever, but because the pirate who died was the one on whom I had placed a curse when he struck me, the word spread amongst the crew that my word was that of the Devil.

One day, as I found out later, in passing the coast of Africa we encountered an English fleet. Below deck we could hear the officers of that fleet challenging the mutineers.

"Who is your captain? Under what flag do you sail?"

No reply that the pirates made would satisfy the English fleet and *The Resurrection* was boarded. Immediately the mutineers came down below and dragged Mr. Walsh and Mr. Summers as hostage on to the deck. They left me below.

"We have taken command of this ship and these shall die if you do not withdraw."

The English fleet withdrew that day and the mutineers held their prisoners on board and kept a watch. Two nights later under cover of dark, longboats from the English fleet drew alongside *The Resurrection* and many sailors boarded her. The pirates were taken without preparation but in the fight they slaughtered Mr. Walsh and Mr. Summers.

The crew of *The Resurrection* was soon subjugated and I was discovered and taken prisoner with the rest, who would not own that I was not one of the mutineers, though I protested my innocence. To the port of London I came, then, in chains.

I await my fate now without being molested, Master Forman. But when we were first taken to the dungeons by Southwark wharf I was beaten and called slave and blackamoor. One or other Jack of the guard would approach me each day with a length of rope and if four of the others held me down they would place it about my neck to measure it for use. I was duly paraded before the council and the learned judges, together with those scoundrels who had led the mutiny on *The Resurrection*.

When my turn came to offer testimony, as you know for you attended the court, I told of the mutiny and said I had no part in it.

I thought it best to conceal from this court the fact that I was a runaway slave from Hispaniola who had been released through the action of the holy Roman priest Father Da Silva.

My companions from on board, the villains and pirates, were held to answer my charge that it was they who had made me captive along with the master of their ship and his first officer and they laughed in ridicule at my words. They had made up below some remarks and each of them separately and together told the tale of how I had eaten the hearts of the victims of our several encounters, that when we overwhelmed a ship and killed the crew, I would board it, cutlass in hand and dig out the hearts of the dying. That I was a practitioner of the dark sciences and played with the Devil with my arts. On the last day of our trial, the wardens of my jail, while bringing me to the face of the judges, poured on my head and shoulders the blood of a pig from a pail and, chained as I was, I could do nothing to restrain them. They presented me before the court in such condition, soaking and red, a sight to offend the most hardened eyes.

That is the story as told to me by W.H. As proof of the truth of it, several times did he show me how he had learnt in the Indies how to make his body live for minutes and even hours without pulse, heartbeat and breath.

66

"Do the men who practice this not die?"

"The breath is not stopped but so slow that no motion can be discerned. The heart and pulse follow. They slow down so that the beat cannot be felt by the fingers of another."

"And you can come out of this as you choose?"

"The mind is fully in control, even more so than going about one's daily business, for the mind has to think about breathing and think about the heartbeat."

It is while we are conversing thus that Master Warden breaks in. A rude interruption.

"Master Forman, I am lost."

He is in great shock and fear. I ask him to sit down and forgetting himself, he sits on the straw and blanket made out for his prisoner, and holds his head.

"Mistress Lilly Camby has disappeared and her clothes are found by the river and a scarf that I had given her is discovered too. My passion for her is public and now it is rumored that I have murdered her."

"And have you?"

"She would not see me and would not keep an appointment with me, but every day I sent her letters, Master Forman, some entreating, some demanding, some begging, some threatening. Perhaps these letters are discovered."

"And have you any knowledge of where she might be and why she has disappeared?"

At this Master Warden looks at W.H. and then shakes his head.

"I have some thoughts on the matter."

"Are you sure you should speak before us?"

"Master Forman, I have come to you with trust and as for

this black fellow I care not, he is to be hung anyway."

There is a silence now. W.H. says not a word. I motion to the warden to leave with me.

As we leave the warden says, "Yes, these wretched men are to be hung the day after tomorrow. My Lord Burghley has signed the warrants for their deaths. But the mob, if the rumors persist, they will hang me with them."

"So our Henry is to be hung at dawn the day after tomorrow on Tower Hill."

The warden nods.

"The executioner is a man in your employ?"

"Yes."

"Good. And do you appoint a physician to pronounce death on the hung man?"

"Yes, I do."

"Then have a black shroud and a coffin prepared for our Henry and now let me take my leave. I must return to him and prepare him for his hanging."

The warden looks on me in amazement.

"And I shall come back to you. Have no fear, Mistress Camby shall be found."

"No, no," He begins to sob. "She shall never be found."

The crowd that gathered on Tower Hill to see the hanging were the usual mob of ragged cut-purses, tapsters, thieves and strumpets who gather at these occasions. They are the gossip of London, the arteries of information. Their whispers make opinion, carrying it far and wide.

The prisoner was brought in a cart to the gallows. There were those who had assembled an hour or two before the hanging to assure themselves a place at the front of the crowd. W.H. was brought from the cart by three executioners and by Master Warden, and the priest stood by to hear any last repentance the prisoner might show.

The black man mounted the scaffold, clad in a shirt of black silk and stood below the hangman's rope which was swept to the side and tied to the gibbet.

His hands were not bound. He looked calm, like an actor who had overcome the nervousness of mounting the stage. He gazed at the crowd.

AN ACCOUNT OF THE HANGING OF LAZARUS AS SEEN BY SIMON FOREMAN

The blackamoor, having climbed the scaffold, then magnificently lifts his hand and summons the priest. The crowd roars. This is more of a circus than they expected.

In a voice that rings through the fields, W.H. says, "I wish to confess myself and make my peace with God the father."

As the priest come forward, W.H. kneels facing the crowd. As the priest crosses himself to hear his confession W.H. begins.

"I wish to confess myself, not of the murders of which I am accused, but of other acts of murder and witchcraft and covetousness. Three sailors did I wish to their deaths by water."

A rumble of voices rises over the heads of the crowd. Some at the back cannot hear what the blackamoor has said and the word is passed.

"I wish to confess myself. I have practiced black arts and made a tryst kept with the Devil which I here renounce. I beg

God's forgiveness and the mercy of Christ. I confess that I have murdered through witchcraft Mistress Lilly Camby of Southwark who practiced the black arts and was in communication with me. She, too, has been transported by water and her clothes left on the banks of the river hard by here. She has been missing these last ten days and I must confess that she has been my lover and has given herself to delight with me and other Devil worshippers. I regret that having repented of my sins I shall never meet her again, as she will surely by now have reached the inner circles of Hell."

At this there are shouts from the crowd. A couple of knaves threw staves and some fighting breaks out further down the field.

W.H. crosses himself and the priest crosses him. Then he mounts the scaffold steps and the hangman takes the halter and puts it round his neck and adjusts the knot so it is hidden behind his head.

To the cries of "crucify him," and "burn the witch at the stake," the order is given by my Master Warden and the trap drops. The body drops and hangs. The crowd surges forward and are kept in check by my Lord Proctor's men.

The ignorant believe that a relic from a dead man's body will bring them luck and I have seen crowds fight for a tuft of a hanged man's head.

The physician pronounces the black man dead and he is put in the deal coffin and removed to the Marshalsea prison, to be buried like all pirates and murderers in unconsecrated ground.

That afternoon Master Warden and I open the coffin and W.H. steps out. I have fresh clothes for him. He removes his silk garment and takes off the harness I have fashioned for him with twelve hooks to hold the leather to his body and one which hooked into the ring on the knot of the noose.

Master Warden has paid the hangman in gold.

"You have perchance saved my life," says the warden.

"In return for my own, no more. Except I have now confessed to a murder I did not commit, to be free of a murder I had no part in," says W.H.

"I asked you nothing before, Master Warden, but where is Lilly Camby in truth?"

"Master Forman, I assure you I know not. My fear is only that she has run away to France in order to escape me, with an adventurer who lodged at her inn. I must say in truth that I threatened her. If she would not love me I would kill her and kill myself. But I am a God-fearing man, sir, I would not kill a fly. Least of all would I kill myself."

"But you allowed me to think you may have killed her rather than tell me that she probably ran away from you?"

"The shame, Master Forman, the shame."

In my lodgings whence I take him, W.H. demands to know why I set him at liberty.

"I suppose I have three motives. First, I would have further conversation with you. I believe we live in a world which mystery begins to yield ground but slowly. I have spoken many times with you and taken down your story and think myself familiar with the outline of it. But I would know more. You are still a mystery to me.

"The second motive I have is to learn what you know of what you assert are simple things. No beast lives without breathing, yet here is a man who can do it for a time.

"And the third reason is that I have never been a clean benefactor to any man in my life. There are many to whom I have predicted one event or the other. Indeed, Lord Burghley himself consults me on the affairs of the state, when is it the right time and month for war and how he should counter the intrigues of one and the treachery of another. None of the advice I give leads to pure gain. Fate is always a mix.

"If a young man asks me to grant him a spell to win a mistress, he wins her and finds that she is a shrew and her mother is better looking. I give him a spell and grant him misery. I once told my Lord Admiral that it was propitious for the fleet to sail. The signs of victory were in the stars, and the fleet sailed. It returned after encounters with the Spaniards, victorious, carrying fewer than half the men they set out with, a couple of chests of gold, their honor intact, their sails and hulls and bodies tattered.

"For you there is a destiny and I drink to myself that I have given you the liberty to follow it. You shall be my assistant in the arts and we shall have conversation till we bleed with knowledge."

Then the Jack says to me that he shall do with his freedom as he pleases. I had better examine the stars again because he will bid me good day.

The slave. The ungrateful slave. But am I not the doctor who has made a profession of ingratitude to nature, probing and examining and using prayer as one would a potion, to see if it works? A corner of myself admires him. Then I put it to him. Would he help me rob the graves of his fellow prisoners who have gone to the gallows without my assistance and will be no more than a worm's supper by now. I would use the bodies for experiment and cut them to see where the humors of wicked men flow. No, he would help me not at all.

I remind him that his face is familiar to the London mob, that he is now an escaped prisoner under threat of the gallows and that the March wind outside will not be any kinder to him than I and the log fire. He says he'll drink to that, drains the cup of sack and he goes. Into the night.

DR. TRENCH CAME THREE TIMES in all to see Mr. B. He was better each time and getting back to normal. The head wound had healed slowly and Rose changed the bandages just as the doctor had instructed her to.

As soon as he recovered from the blow, the old man started questioning Rose about how the doctor got to the house.

She told him that she didn't give out the address and he looked satisfied. Of course by now Dr. Trench knew where he lived and arrived from the Tube station on foot.

"She was a very attractive woman, you know, handsome and most accomplished. A person of great culture, my dear Rose."

"She's still good-looking," Rose said.

"A bit overtaken," said the old man, "but she is the only one I can trust. She says she's taken on another doctor in her practice."

Rose was dying to ask him where he made the acquaintance of Dr. Trench.

All the old man would say was, "I have known her for many years now and she never breaks promises. I broke my promise to her, though."

"What promise was that?"

The old man thought for a long while.

"Rosey my dear, Dr. Trench wanted to marry me, you know. I promised her I would. That was in another country. Then everything changed and I couldn't keep my promise. Some day I'll tell you. But first we have to finish our story."

"Did she ever get married to anyone else?"

"I was hoping she wouldn't."

"You just wanted her to remain a spinster and wait for you?"

This was the first impudent thing she had ever asked the old man, but he didn't seem to notice or mind.

"No, no, she did get hold of a feller as a matter of fact. She married a useless hustler called Beddie Eddie. That's what they called him, because he was a ladies' man and was always in and out of bed with almost anyone. Scoundrel. Lived off her and ran off with an Australian."

IT IS THE DAY of tricks and the day when fools come into the street to declare their grand plans and to defy the stars with boasting. The first signs I hear of stirring in the streets of Southwark beneath my window are the cries of advertisement for a play by the Lord Admiral's Men, *The Entertainment Of The Jew Of Malta.*

It is a day certainly governed by the Fates because no sooner has this cry dissolved in the wakening sounds of the city than there is a knock upon my door and a messenger comes with a summons written in a hand with great flourish.

It is from Sir Edward Coke, known here in the city as the eyes and ears of my Lord Burghley and now Solicitor General for the Queen. I have attended my Lord Burghley many a time and have done him service carrying him intelligence of things in the underworlds of London — the worlds of cut-throats and taverners and players.

I shall go as soon as I can, I reply. This shall not be soon enough says the messenger, he is instructed to take me with him. I get dressed in haste and follow the man to Westminster.

To my heart and this paper the truth is consigned. Sir Edward is seated in a chair of grand decoration. He paces the room.

He is a man of few words and speaks to the vapors of the room rather than to my ears. It is as though the walls listen to him. He is least concerned whether I look at him as he speaks.

"Master Forman, you have powers. Arts."

"God willing, I am a man of piety."

I must be careful of any answer I give him. This man has at his command an army of spies, here and abroad. Like caterpillars they hide under leaves and eat at the roots and branches.

It is said that he has no friends. Those he had, he has accused of treason and sent them to their death for his own political advantage. With humble men such as myself he would do as he does with house flies.

"Have no fear. I have sent men to their death and I have sent other men whom I should have sent to their death to the service of the Queen."

I begin to read his mind. With the practice of the art of foretelling the future comes naturally the practice of knowing a personality, reading the mind's construction in the face.

Sir Edward comes to the matter. There is growing a faction in the kingdom of godless men with power near to the throne. Lord Burghley is most concerned that these men will attempt to stir up the common consciousness against the Queen and the faith. It is known that they are full of treason and may try and create an incident in the city by provoking the mob to some ungodly act.

And how is that to be done? I ask. It is difficult enough to force one being to love another using all the arts of God and the Devil at my command. How is it possible to raise so many voices against our good and gracious Queen?

"You come to the point, Master Forman. In the circle of these men of power are two or three idle educated upstarts.

They call themselves writers of plays and under this guise spread all manner of rebellion and sedition and implant ideas in the heads of the general mob, which ideas are then become like coin to pass from one to the other and join the general traffic of hands.''

''Except, my lord, that this coin would not bear the face of our gracious queen?''

Sir Edward nods. He is uncomfortable with any flourish of speech from the likes of me. Then he says, ''It shall be your embassy to find them out and bring back intelligence of their blasphemy, their treason, their plans, plots, intentions, all, to us. We shall make an example of a few. The chief amongst them is one Marley or Marlowe.''

And this very morning it was that I heard the name, proclaimed as the writer of *The Jew Of Malta*. Which play I resolve to go and see in order that through this company of actors, the Lord Admiral's Men, I may encounter this Christopher Marlowe.

Men love to have power over other men. It is like as to the satisfaction of enchantment, of knowing that one's beloved holds in the mind a portrait, to be caressed with thought. The power of spells is uncertain. I myself, who have conjured the dead, scarcely know if I have any belief in the dead or in the Almighty.

As I go about London I become aware that it is dangerous to work for Sir Edward. He is a man of secrets, it is said, and he keeps those secrets by killing the bearers of them. To put it plainly, he gets men and women to work for him and then disposes of them. To succeed for Sir Edward is to fail oneself. He rewards informers with a bag of coins and has them killed and looted as soon as he pleases by other spies who then go, in this never-ending chain, to their own deaths. In this maze I am trapped. I wish I had never set eyes on the dog. To inform is fatal and not to inform is also fatal.

I have come close to tracking down his infernal Marlowe, this man of cheek, of plays and stories and devils embroidered in them. Fie! I have studied devils forty years and know them well. Their ways, their demands, their uses for men and women. And yet there are these so-called playwrights and poets in Southwark who come from the universities and in some boyish fit pretend that they have discovered the secrets we have sacrificed our lives to find. Boys! It is but a fashion with them, the Devil, the arts, the evils. Even blasphemy.

The fellow Marlowe has a reputation somewhat different from these other playwrights and poets and men of birth, breeding and devilish adventure in the colleges. His very being scoffs at all divinity and brings other men to heel with the power of argument.

I have this day sat eleven hours in the tavern of Mistress Near. In this tavern there is a ruffian who with pieces of coal will trace on the floor-stones of the yard the likeness of any person known to him. I ask him to conjure with his memory and draw the face and body of this Marlowe. The ruffian waits to be paid. Then from the emptiness on the stones, in quick and thick strokes, there emerges the face. Thick eyebrows asserting the stare and puzzlement in the eyes which the mouth opposes, being certain of itself and arrogant in quick twists and smiles. There is command in the face.

Mine is but a sad face, whose melancholy hangs in its cheeks, dragging my lower eyelids down. It is age. I am never so young as him and that, too, makes me envious.

Does this boy then believe in the Devil? I ask myself how

blasphemous is the fellow, in truth? I am a man of science. Let us examine the question of Marlowe. Or of all belief.

Does my Lord Francis Drake believe the world is round, or my Lord Raleigh, who would set sail for all the unknown world in search of — what? Gold. On examination it would be found that Sir Walter neither believes the world is round nor flat. He has heard the Portuguese assess and make many maps of navigation upon this roundness, but he cares not for the disputation. Or put it another way. He cares more that it is round so that he can get his hands on the gold in some other round part.

So likewise with Marlowe. He blasphemes because it helps him get on in this society of fashion, playwrighting, vanity.

And Sir Walter wants not the gold for any purpose but that he may have power over men. And I want not the grace of the spirits, the help of the dead, the workings of my science, of all the world, of the spheres, the smallest atom, but that I may have power over men.

To spy is a small and sly satisfaction of this power. Given to me by Sir Edward, who glows with the power he has from closeness to the throne. I have stolen some heat from him and hold it, as savages do pots of coals to their bellies and bosoms and go about with their warmth enfolded. It is a secret power the watcher has of knowing he is commissioned to watch. And yet it is not power itself. It is wanting the woman you imagine rather than the woman you have.

I have seen the play *The Jew Of Malta* and have spent the day in trying to reproduce in every word and through every scene what I saw on stage.

I visit the Marshalsea prison. I am given entrance by my friend Master Warden. Of W.H. we say nothing. He is eternally grateful to me for the way we have disposed of the Lilly Camby affair, because when she was declared as having disappeared, many witnesses came forward to say that she had been bewitched by a black man who was hung for the crime. No suspicion has come his way. I wish to record and watch over the habits and the diet of those who are condemned by the courts and observe their dispositions.

There is a young man of very hasty temper, a man called John Cocke who has been condemned for the murder of his own family. He is a wretch who has no regrets and no repentance passes his lips. He is willing to speak to me freely. The warden tells me that he is kept from the other prisoners lest they do him harm. He boasts of his deeds and has no fear of the gallows. When he is allowed out of his cells and passes the yard there is a general clamor as even among prisoners there are ranks and order and at the bottom stands the man who has killed his own.

I have begun a small work on this man's confession. He speaks to me because I tell him I will write it down and other men will read it.

His story is a sad one but we must here press on with the tale of Master Marlowe.

JUNE 3RD

I attend the performance of *Romulus And Remus* by one Anthony Munday written for the Admiral's Men and performed for six days at The Globe. It is a play concerning the Pope and is a most vicious attack on the enemies of England and the

Queen. In the play the city of Rome and the foundation of the Romanist church are the work of the Devil, who has as his agent the twins to whom the building of Rome, the city, is given in the ancient books. Romulus and Remus dispute on stage what they want to make of the citadel they have built. Remus says it will be a home for the Devil for the centuries to come. It is a clever play and shows the Pope to be a puppet of the princes who appoint him.

In the evening I am at the Marston Arms where the Admiral's Men take their leisure and where many of the theatrical world congregate.

This day *Romulus And Remus* has been a great success. Many from the court at Greenwich have come by barge up the river to see the play. Master Munday is well pleased with the praise of the high and the low who have gathered after the performance and he struts about the tavern like a cock who has a ten-foot cockscomb.

In comes Master Marlowe attended by three or four who do regularly drink and then venture into some argument or dispute. The ruffian's drawing was good. It is the very man from that likeness.

Master Marlowe proceeds to open his purse and calls for drink for the whole company.

"What are we celebrating, Master Kit?" asks one of Munday's company.

"Not celebrating, but drowning sorrow," says Marlowe.

"Sorrow for what?" asks Mr. Munday. "Has your Muse died?"

"No," protests Master Marlowe, "sorrow that a strumpet of a play should disguise herself as a Muse and strut the boards of The Globe."

There is now a silence in the tavern. Master Marlowe is known to be quick of temper and the rumor is that he is not well-pleased that his own play has been replaced in favor by this one of *Romulus And Remus*.

"The audience liked it well enough," says a supporter of Master Munday.

"No doubt they would," replies Marlowe. "It is the first I have seen of an audience paid to watch a play rather than paying. A sad day when spies and writers of such dull disputes can call themselves playwrights."

"Better these than plotters who hide their purpose in riddles," says Master Munday, "which purpose shall be found out and punished."

Too much for Master Marlowe.

"My riddles, Munday, will last through Tuesday unto the next Sunday. You are nothing but a ratcatcher and a slave first of Lord Dudley and now to whoever will bid most highest for you. You sell your tongue and I marvel at the buyers of so dead and dull a thing."

There is laughter in the tavern and one of Munday's men steps forward to grab Marlowe by the shoulder, but he is struck by one of Marlowe's friends whom I know to be Ingram Frizer, one of Lord Walsingham's servants.

Another of Marlowe's friends, who have come there to cause a fight, picks up a stool and hurls it at Munday's group. There are shouts of coward and three or four swords are drawn but the Marlowe faction withdraws, being completely outnumbered. They go with the satisfaction that they have laid a territory to waste.

I go again to The Globe, to see *Edward II* by Master Marlowe himself. It is a most disturbing spectacle and I must go again to take a note of all that is said.

In the course of the play the prince is murdered with hot irons being forced into his body through the anus to burn out his insides. I have made a study of torture and am of the opinion that this Kit Marlowe has made invention of his own take the place of history. He must have a purpose.

Amongst the mob of London, the play is even more popular than the last offering by the Admiral's Men from Master Munday. Marlowe has no following among the lords and ladies of the court but many young men from the Inns attend the play on all days and feast and drink with Master Marlowe after the performances.

I note one curious fact. A torturer appears in the play wearing a mask and says but two words. Somewhere I, who have an ear for voices, know the movements of this masked figure. But many vagrants and adventurers join the acting companies for a week or for the duration of but one performance so it may be that I am much mistaken.

After the performance I repair to the Marston Arms. I cannot see Master Marlowe. The masked man is there, still wearing his mask which covers the top of his face. On his head he wears a cap to hide the cut of his hair. The lower part of his face is greased and is colored black. There are of course diverse blackamoors in London and some in the playhouses and acting companies. I keep a steady ear out and when the players buy this masked man a drink they refer to him as "Lazarus." Arisen from the dead again? Yes. It is he. I will not approach him. I have Master Marlowe to seek and I have too many questions and too much business with Mr. W.H. who now seems to call himself Lazarus.

I spent till midnight hunting the taverns of Southwark for Marlowe, but he is nowhere to be found.

In the taverns the play is part of the talk, together with prattle of who is the mistress of whom.

I have a trained ear for the overhearing of the talk of others. A great deal may be learnt of general opinion in a place of public gathering by this means. The young gentlemen remark that it is now lawful to kill the Kings of England even in stage mockery. Neither should the King be shown as weak and bringing upon himself the revenge of traitors. One of the gentlemen protests that he has heard Master Marlowe, whom he knows well, say that only fools and knaves who wish to profit by other men's foolishness believe in Almighty God.

I am sent for by Sir Edward Coke and report what I have seen and heard. It is not enough information on which to hang a man or to pass sentence of heresy or treason upon him.

"You have had no conference with Marlowe?"

"Not yet, my lord."

"It is now important that one or two of the heretics be brought to trial," Sir Edward says and he puts a coin of silver, wet with his sweat, into my palm.

I attend the final performance of *Edward II*. I have my notebook and quill and I place my book upon my knee at the side of the stage and observe from there.

Half-way through the performance a fellow challenges me and asks me to go with him. I am asked to step into a tent on the ground outside The Globe. Unmistakably, there is Kit Marlowe, dark and handsome on a stool.

"Master Forman," he says, and as I am about to protest at his knowledge of my name, "we have spies too."

"You may," I say, "but what is the purpose of summoning me here?"

"Pray what is the purpose for which you note down the words of my characters?"

"I am fond of study."

"Oh we know that, Master Forman, your reputation as a doctor is very wide. But why make enquiry from my friends of what I say and where I am to be found?"

"Only, sir, in order to offer words of admiration for the fine plays you have presented."

"This bastard lies as readily as a pig squeals," he says to his companions, who laugh. "Please forgive me, Master Forman. A man does not like to be spied upon."

"I have no reason to forgive, not being offended," I say.

"Very good, then. Will you drink with us? Give Master Forman some wine. It is the best French wine."

I thank him and take the seat that is offered.

"I too am a student of the human mind, Master Forman. I grant you I don't go to the lengths as we hear you do of taking brains from bodies and weighing them and then squeezing the blood from them to weigh them again, but in my way I am a humble student."

"Indeed, sir."

"And having studied you for two minutes, I know that you do what you do against me for gain."

I venture no word.

"Well, being a student of nature I say that profit can be replaced by higher profit. In other words, if you are being paid to spy on me, I shall pay you double the amount not to spy on me."

"I do not spy on you, sir," I protest, and then seeing that it would profit me more to befriend this gentleman, I continue, "for any payment or gold."

"Then why do you spy on me?"

"In the hope of winning your confidence, sir."

"How so?"

"My studies in human nature tell me that those you fear as enemies, you would readily embrace as friends, if they show but a sign of giving up their enmity."

"Master Forman, you have studied wisely. For my part I would say that we love to embrace that which we most fear. To make a friend of someone who would harm us most."

"Your words clothe my naked thought, sir."

He is amused. "You know Forman, I was sent to school in Canterbury and hated attending it. There were great bullies in that school who would take the younger boys for maidens. I feared them and when I grew to seniority in the school myself, was careful to be the opposite of these brutes. And yet sometimes I wonder whether in some dark place in my mind the longing to be as hateful does not lurk."

"I am sure it has no place in your character, Master Marlowe."

"But the urge to speak plainly does."

"Then so you must."

"With a little help from you. You are a man of magic and one who has probed other worlds."

"You flatter me, sir."

"I have even heard that you have made the dead walk again."

"No, sir, as you must know this is beyond the prospect of magic. It has never been done."

Master Marlowe's interest sharpens.

"Never? Not by Jesus Christ as the gospels tell us?"

I search his face and make no reply.

"Never. Never is good. It is also sacrilege. I suppose you say it to draw me out? So that you may swear to Sir Edward and before the Privy Council that Marlowe, Christopher Marlowe, did blaspheme and rail against the gospels and Jesus Christ whom he said performed no miracle and died a mortal. Justly punished for impudence."

"That was not my intention."

"Well even if it was, I didn't step into your trap. I don't love the sound of my own syllables so much. But you did some talking. Denied the miracles. That puts you in danger."

"Not when you are the only witness, Master Marlowe."

"These bastards would sell their servants if it were to their advantage. But you are wrong. I am not the only witness."

He holds his head up and commands: "My dearest boy, come and meet your savior!"

Fresh from the performance, from the black flap of the tent steps the masked man, the executioner as was. Now of course I am certain.

Henry removes his mask.

"How did it go?" asks Marlowe.

"They applauded till their echo was exhausted."

Pleasure flicks over Marlowe's face. Then Henry bends down and gives Marlowe a kiss. On the lips.

Marlowe accepts it with passion and turns to me again.

"I believe you have the pleasure of knowing my Lazarus.

He who has risen because of you from the dead. Of course since we call him that, we must call you Jesu. He has told me the story. You wouldn't want to be called Jesus, would you, Master Forman?"

"No."

"Let me then tell you why we called you here. Firstly to stop you spying on me, though I cannot pay you more money than my Lord Burghley. And then to tell you that the noose is tightening anyway. You are not alone in your quest. Thirty or forty gentlemen and noblemen are under suspicion and will soon be swept away in inquisitions and trials where false witness will be as common as peacocks in paradise."

"I never thought I was alone commissioned to find information. I must protest, though that I have never been approached to perjure myself."

"As we said, Master Forman, there is nothing we can pay you, but we would ask you, holding our payment to the future as a deep and honor-bound debt, to find out the names and movements of those who have been set to spy on us."

"I know I haven't paid my own life's debt to you, Master Forman," says the black man, "but I haven't forgotten. There was a reason for walking away from you. Because you wanted me to tell you what I didn't know. You saw me, Master Forman as a black man and for me, that escape from the gallows was like a mirror shattering. I would never see that image again. I was going to be new. My life had to be new."

"My dear Lazarus — if that is the name to which you now answer — I am not here to gain anything from you. I have already been told. I am here to spy on Master Marlowe, but I tell you in truth I can show you instead a way of escape for him."

"And why would you do that for me?" asks Master Marlowe.

"Because you are, sir, a poet and an artist," say I.

Master Marlowe bows low to me and then I to him. It is a game we play.

"There are other spies set to catch me, Master Forman."

"Yes, Master Marlowe. But I am the cleverest."

ONE MORNING Rose turned up and heard the old man clapping. Distinct, single claps, four times then five. She went up the stairs and into his room without knocking.

"Damn moths," Mr. B said, "one of the Old Testament plagues, Rosey, they'll eat everything."

He was standing on the bed. The wardrobe was open and he was clapping his hands in the air, intent on smashing the moths which Rose couldn't see.

"Don't just stand there, man, get them out of the wardrobe!"

Rose looked in the wardrobe. As she shook the clothes two or three moths flew out. The old man got excited.

"See, I told you so, I'm not going senile, child, bloody moths. Get some stuff, spray, kill them without mercy. No prisoners."

"They must have a nest in here," Rose said.

"Take all the stuff out."

Rose took the clothes out, sweaters, suits, coats. At the end of the rail was an old ankle-length fur coat and as Rose touched it to pull it out, handfuls of fur came away in her fist.

"Yuck. This fur coat is rotting."

"Show me," the old man demanded.

Rose took the coat over to the bed. It was shedding fur all the way. She held it at arm's length.

"That's what's making the moths. This coat's dead."

"Hmm." The old man wasn't pleased. "I suppose you must throw it away. I loved it, man, it was my favorite thing."

"Did you wear it here?"

"In Switzerland, I bought it in Zurich," the old man said absently. He had let this slip and Rose knew he regretted having said it. Mr. B took the coat and turned out the pockets. Out of one of them came an old photograph.

"How the hell did this stay in here?"

Rose fetched a black plastic bag and dumped the coat in it. The photograph was on the bed as she dusted the fur off it. It was of the old man, maybe years ago, with a hat at an angle, wearing the same coat. He was part of a group that had had their photograph taken, some African-looking men with thick blanketlike shawls wrapped around their shoulders.

When Rose looked again the old man was tucking the photograph under his pillow and he didn't mention it further. The next morning when she was making the bed she noticed that he had stowed it away.

Rose dusted the cupboard out, put some moth balls in it and put the clothes back.

The Diary Of Simon Forman

AS IT PERTAINS TO THE FATE OF
CHRISTOPHER MARLOWE, GENT.

I am summoned to the Marshalsea. There has been a death and Master Warden returns my favors by calling me. I have left instructions with him.

I need the body for my studies and the warden calls me when there is no one who would claim the carcass of a wretch.

"You have been at the plays, Master Forman?"

"And at work. And yourself?"

"I busy myself with preparing the prison. Many great men will pass through it soon, I am told. Several gentlemen are accused of plotting. Any day now the eagle will swoop."

I say nothing of my commission to spy.

"How do you know this?"

"Ah, Master Forman. I only tell you this in the strictest trust and in order that you may protect yourself. There is a gentleman called Anthony Bacon who has recently been appointed a member of parliament, where of course he is never to be found. This gentleman has been employed as a spy and was making, through other acquaintance of mine, some enquiries. Your name came up."

"My name? Indeed?"

"Yes, Master Forman. And I did not deny I knew you. But I said you were a master of physic and no witch or wizard."

"And they were hunting witches?"

"The hunt goes forward for all sorts of creature. Like fish in the sea they are to be netted."

"And would there be heretics and devil-worshippers amongst them?"

Master Warden nods.

"One Master Marlowe, perhaps?"

He is struck by the name and looks in my face.

I press a coin in his hand. "Keep me informed. Now to your dead body. I didn't know there was an execution today."

"Not a hanging. Did you require that the body be whole?"

He looks worried. "Nay, Master Forman, there has been a stabbing here and a death of a man of no consequence. He was to be executed in the weeks to come, but I dare say no one in this God's creation will regret his passing."

We walked through the prison to the dungeon chambers. There laid out on a slab of wood like a slaughtered animal was John Cocke.

I examined the body. It was cut and still unclean. The blood had poured out of the top of the right eye where it seems a sharp instrument had pierced the skin and smashed through the bone of the forehead, the hood of the eye.

"How did this happen?"

"The other prisoners. One killed him with a cobbler's spike when they passed his cell and he jeered at them. They pressed him to the bars and through the frame stabbed him till he fell. One blow through the eye."

"So I see. Was he stabbed anywhere else or did this blow do for him? Can you get me the instrument which killed him? I would wish to compare the depth to which the iron was thrust."

"I have it."

"I'll give you an extra shilling," I said, knowing what his hesitation meant. "I still have to protect myself. Towards dark, by the usual method."

The prospect of a fresh body was always exciting and I had to prime myself to work with lamp and blade through the night before the body went stale. I would return at night in the guise of a carter with sacks of flour and carry the covered body away. The carter who would lend me cart and harness and bags could be found amongst the traders of Cheapside. I had to hurry.

I crossed London Bridge and was thinking to myself of the Tower and the men locked up in there awaiting execution. It put me in mind of Master Marlowe. Just then on the bridge I caught sight of one of the actors from the Lord Chamberlain's players. A fellow from Warwickshire whom I had met in the company of Master Marlowe. On the night I saw Kit Marlowe attack the playwright Munday, this fellow had spoken to me. Now he was drunk and making progress in the opposite direction with uncertain step. On recognizing me he accosted me.

"Master Forman. It is my good fortune to meet you thus

suspended between north and south with only the river below us."

"Yes, Master Shakespeare," I said, intending to hurry on.

"Might I trouble you for a loan of a half-crown? I shall pay it back when my engagement with the Admiral's company begins tomorrow. Be sure not to miss the performance and you shall have your money. An excellent return of Kyd's *Spanish Tragedy* to Shoreditch."

"Yes, Master Marlowe spoke highly of it and he speaks highly of very few playwrights."

"Marlowe is uncommonly generous and uncommonly clever," said the fellow. "I would have had the shilling from him had he not been abroad."

"Abroad?" I enquired.

"Ah yes, at least," and he placed his fingers on his lips, "as far as my Lord Walsingham's in Chiselhurst, which is never so far as Stratford."

I gave him a shilling on the promise of return and hurried over the bridge. Now I was not of a mind to hire a cart, but indeed to get hold of a horse.

I wanted to get to Chiselhurst.

I rode through the evening and stopped at a tavern in Deptford to refresh myself and ask the way. This inn had a yard and there were travelers' rooms for rest above.

Not many were about and I remarked this, whereupon the landlady, one Mistress Eleanor Bull, said it was on account of the plague. It had taken Deptford badly and many stayed at home.

I said it had taken us badly too in Southwark and though I was a doctor of physic I had sent my family to Salisbury to preserve them.

As I rode out she bade me a good night and hoped she would see me again. Especially if I had a cure for the plague. The others of the company laughed at her boldness and I promised I would take refreshment there again on my journey back on the morrow.

I arrived at Lord Walsingham's before midnight. A light was still to be seen as I walked my horse before the house. Like an apparition I looked in and before me in the room saw five young men before a log fire, two of them wrestling in jest and the other three watching. The one was Master Lazarus, wrestling with another of the house and of those on the floor one was Master Marlowe. I waited at the window, watching till Lazarus had his opponent on his back. The others made slow move to applaud.

I knocked at the window and at first they didn't hear me for the crackling of the logs but soon one young man turned and declared that he had seen a ghost. One of the others turned and on looking me in the face clapped to call a servant, to enquire who was about.

I informed the serving man that I was an acquaintance of his guests and he asked my name and announced me, whereupon Master Marlowe himself came to escort me in.

He was puzzled.

"What brings you to my Lord Walsingham's? He himself is in France."

"I seek you out, sir."

"But how did you know I was here?"

"One of the actors, sir, much under the influence of wine."

"Ah, only two men know where we are and that, by the sound of him, will be Master Shakespeare."

I said he was correct. He motioned me into the room

and sent for more drink, that I may be refreshed.

"You must have had a merry ride? But you must tell me to what I owe this visit."

I indicated with the merest motion of my head that the others prevented me from speaking my mind.

"You should speak," said Marlowe, "these men, all are dear to me. Indeed I am here to seek the protection of Lord Walsingham, who has ever been cousin to me. In London we heard of my imminent arrest and I thought then, yesterday, of you and whether you had intelligence of it."

"I heard of it today, and I have come to suggest a route of escape."

"I have spoken with friends and I would escape to France but I heard Lord Burghley's spies are already watching the gates of this very house. They have full knowledge of your coming and going. This time I am not to escape alive."

He spoke as though he cared not for the life of which he spoke.

"Master Marlowe, I have come to suggest the contrary and am heartened to find you among friends, for we shall need friends. All save Master Lazarus, who being a wanted man himself, cannot assist."

With that we withdrew to a chamber beyond and I explained my purpose. Master Marlowe was pensive, but thoughtful and kind he offered me lodgings for the night and instructed that my horse be stabled.

MAY 30, 1593

I ride back to London in the morning and am followed in a closed coach by Master Lazarus. We meet at my lodgings in

Southwark and then proceed together to Cheapside for the hire of the cart and to acquire three casks of ale from the brewery at Blackfriars.

We sit in my lodgings till dusk and then taking the cart, having disguised ourselves in the clothes of serving men, we proceed to Marshalsea. There we load the body of John Cocke on to the cart and carry it home under the flour sacking. In the yard of my household we unload the body.

"I see what you mean," says Master Lazarus on looking upon the face of the dead man.

"And yet it will need some dressing. Did you say my Lord Walsingham returns from France tonight with his son?"

Lazarus nods. On the hour of ten we get the body on to the cart again and loading it with the barrels of ale which we tie on to the body, we start on our way to Deptford, Lazarus, hooded, pushing the cart of ale and I on the horse, pretending no acquaintance with him.

By eleven we were in Deptford in the yard of the inn owned by Mistress Eleanor Bull, the very same in which I had rested on the way to Chiselhurst. It was the hour we had appointed. I alighted from my horse. The play had no rehearsal. As I alighted a mighty scream went up from inside the tavern. Several people on the thoroughfare outside paused, their blood chilled. A man screaming into the night and then the sound of other shouts.

The mistress of the house dashed out of it just as I walked to the lit door. She clung to my cloak.

"Good doctor. There has been murder. Blood, everywhere blood." And she fell to the ground at my feet, her eyes rolling. I have seen many an actor play at being the gentle lady fainting for fear or love, but Mistress Bull was the best.

"Someone look to this lady. I will see who is wounded within."

I entered. As planned, in the taproom stood Nicholas Skeres, Robert Poley and Ingram Frizer, the three youths who were with Master Marlowe in Chiselhurst. Under the table, next to the door to the yard lay Master Marlowe himself. They glanced at me as I walked in.

Others were now pressing to enter the taproom from the street and from elsewhere in the tavern. Master Marlowe stood and opened the door to the yard and Lazarus and Frizer deftly pulled in the body of John Cocke.

Master Marlowe disappeared, and with him Lazarus.

Now it was my turn. Like an actor on a stage I rushed to the entrance and held my hand up to the crowd that pressed there.

"I am a physician. A man has been murdered. Hold the crowd back. See that no man leaves this chamber for within here is the man who held the knife."

From the shirt of John Cocke, Ingram Frizer pulled the knife we had bloodied and cast it on the floor.

Masters Skeres and Poley apprehended Ingram and held him down, crying, "We have the villain."

"Who is the victim?" I enquired of them.

"It is Master Christopher Marlowe. A cousin of Lord Walsingham's. We are servants of Lord Walsingham, and there was a quarrel between us about the reckoning of the meal we have had, as we were traveling together. There was a fight. Mistress Bull saw it, sir."

"Do not remove the body, it is illegal," I said. "We must inform the local coroner and an inquest must be held."

"Where shall we leave this corpse?" enquired Mistress Bull.

"I should leave it where it has come to rest," I said.

I stay the night at Deptford with the body now thought to be that of Christopher Marlowe. Men are summoned to take it to a place of rest and another is sent to fetch those of Lord Walsingham's household who will testify at the inquest the next morning.

The inquest is held with twelve men of the jury who don't know Christopher Marlowe from Tamburlaine. The trick is with Lord Walsingham, who attends the inquest himself. The color of the hair is identical and we sheared the length of Cocke's hair to that of Kit Marlowe's, which was shorter and cut like that of a gentleman.

One who has made a study of features knows that there are two systems in the structure of the face. There are the eyes and the cheeks and the forehead, taking in the eyebrows and their thickness or thinness. Then there is the jaw and the chin and thus the shape of the mouth where the two bone formations meet. We may look at the top half of two faces and see a similarity. Or we may notice the same of the jaw section. Some children take after their fathers for the top and their mothers for the bottom.

It was true that the lower half of poor John Cocke's face could have been that of Kit Marlowe. The same jaw and the same insolent mouth. The top half would differ, but in this case it was full of blood and I had deviled the wound about to be deeper than it was at first, so as to destroy the eyebrows and disguise with a clot of blood the shape of the bridge of the nose.

I am called by the inquest to pronounce the subject dead.

"I pronounce him dead. And gentlemen of the jury, as someone who has been to a hundred inquests and not been moved, I must declare that Master Marlowe was known to me. He resided hard by me and was a great poet and playwright. May his soul rest in peace."

"You were not asked to give identification," says the coroner. "You were called for evidence as to death."

"And yet I was moved to give it sir, forgive me. Who better can identify this poor man?" With this I draw a kerchief.

"Why, my Lord Walsingham was called for this purpose."

The coroner smiles. No doubt the slave is looking for preference from milord.

Lord Walsingham steps forward. He has just come from his journeys and this is a burden to him.

I step out and cover the top half of the face of John Cocke.

"My lord, there was no need to call you to this unpleasant duty. I fear if he was any kin to you, you will not desire to look upon this."

"I shall look. Yes, that's Christopher Marlowe. Certain. But remove the kerchief, let me look at the wound, man."

I move the kerchief to the lower half of the face, so only the botched top is seen.

"A nasty wound. Is Ingram Frizer here?" Lord Walsingham demands.

"He is here and soon we shall hear the cause of the brawl and of this death, your lordship," sings the coroner.

When the verdict of death by misadventure of Christopher Marlowe is pronounced by the jurors, Lord Walsingham asks the court for the protection of Ingram Frizer, his servant.

"He shall be dealt with within the law. I shall see to it,"

says Lord Walsingham, and no commoner dares to challenge him.

I have to hide Marlowe for several days. He is there with Lazarus when I return to my lodgings that night. Lazarus has brought in some fine French wine, from where one knows not.

"We must drink to your second miracle, Master Forman, you have now raised more bodies than Christ himself."

I drink.

"It is not done yet. We have to get you out of England."

"We shall accomplish that, Master Forman. Now to bed? But one more thing. I am sure my body won't be allowed to rest in peace in Deptford. My friends, my relatives will want the coffin and remains returned to Canterbury. Or perhaps my college, Corpus at Cambridge, will have it for their churchyard."

"But not being men of science they won't open the coffin to find poor unfortunate Master Cocke?"

FOR TWO DAYS there was rioting in Brixton. Some of the young people set fire to two police cars and to a shop and there were running battles on the streets between youth and police. The bus that Rose was in had to go on the side roads.

When she got to Mr. B's he was watching the riot as it happened on television. She was surprised to find the Inspector and the other man, his assistant, crowding around the same TV, standing behind Mr. B and watching the police run through the streets and form cordons. The reporter on TV, a young white man, was speaking to people who were standing around, spectators at a riot.

"This is terrific stuff Rosey, terrific stuff. They have them on the run, these boys." The old man was wickedly excited.

"It's not so terrific when they try and burn down the bus you are sitting in."

"These fellers have been turning up every half hour to talk nonsense. Half of them are saying these young blacks are criminals and have to be brought to book. The other half are saying they are unemployed and driven to desperation. How did it really start?"

"Some of the boys on my estate were there," said Rose. The Ullah boys had come back from school when the riot started and the older guys from the estate were gossiping in the courtyard the previous evening.

"A policeman outside a betting shop stopped two young men and told them that he was charging them with illegal parking. They abused him and when he called for assistance on his radio to arrest them, they took his radio away and slapped him. The squad cars passing by arrested them and all the people from the betting shop came out and fought a battle with the two or three squad cars of police who called for reinforcements. They arrived and so did reinforcements from the street. Doesn't take much, does it?"

"Are we safe here?" The old man turned to the Inspector.

"I think we are."

"Well you better stay in the spare room till it blows over," he said to Rose. "We can't have your bus burnt down with you in it."

From The Diary Of Simon Forman

JUNE 6, 1593

To the presence of Sir Edward Coke. He is a most particular gentleman. He has heard of the accidental death in a quarrel of Christopher Marlowe and has already questioned Ingram Frizer, to whom he has offered a pardon. Frizer has played his part well.

Sir Edward knows something of my part in the inquest and asks how I came to be at such an event.

"I feared that Marlowe was preparing to flee the country and accordingly had him followed and trailed. I was then brought intelligence of his being in a brawl in a tavern and that very night went to Deptford and found that his wound had been fatal to him, may God have mercy on his soul."

"A hopeless prayer, I fear," says Sir Edward.

He pays me in coin for my troubles and says he will keep it in mind that I have done the state some service.

I return to Southwark by way of Shoreditch and on the route use the merest part of my gain to buy some meat and bread for the two fugitives who are now in my care. They must soon leave, as it spells danger for them and me.

Master Marlowe has sent Lazarus to secure passage to France on a ship. He leaves from Southampton on the morrow.

In the night I hear them converse. The walls of my lodgings are thin and Master Marlowe and Lazarus share a bedchamber, a room in which are kept several of my medicines and preparations. There are in it two couches and they use them, I fear, to sleep on. It is these same couches I use to place bodies upon, when cutting them to discover their secrets. The blackamoor says he must go with Marlowe to France.

Thus Master Marlowe: "That would be full of danger. We cannot travel together. When I am settled there I shall send for you."

Robert Poley calls for Master Marlowe at daybreak and they are gone. He carries but one bag of papers and possessions.

Lazarus tells me he will keep his part of the bargain. He has to find lodgings and employment for himself. He has the idea that he can hold a spear or swing an axe in Cuthbert Burbage's Theatre with the Chamberlain's Men. He is known to the Admiral's Men and to Master Edward Alleyn but they know of his closeness to Master Marlowe and he does not wish to attract any curious eyes or ears. He wants no questioning on the affair. He must learn to live as the world does, without one Kit Marlowe.

Lazarus, on Kit's advice, is to seek employment with Master Burbage, who is quick of temper and does not make friends fast. He has a letter from the poor departed Marlowe which he can show to Master Burbage, asking that he be given humble and secret employment as he is a good actor.

"So Burbage gets a letter from beyond the grave. It will surely hold his attention. Perhaps you should present it to Master Alleyn of the Admiral's Men. He is known to me as a man of great superstition, one who crosses himself if he be awake when the cock crows."

With this Lazarus goes.

THE STORY OF the blackamoor and Marlowe kept Rose
writing late into each night. She'd copy what Mr. B dictated
in longhand, but very fast and take it home to type. Between
Mr. B's and home she'd visit the hospital.

Rose knew all the nurses and workers on the wards, the re-
ceptionists and even a couple of the ambulance men. One
evening she was walking down a crowded corridor with people almost in queues coming and going from the lifts and
stairs to the wards, when she thought she saw the young man,
Herbert, walking the other way, with a rolled-up newspaper
in his hand. He didn't look at her, though Rose had the feeling that he noticed her as he passed.

Rose went to her mother's bed in the corner of the ward.
She kissed her. There was a bouquet of flowers in the vase on
the locker and an unopened box of dates.

"Who's been to see you?"

Rose could see from the doubt that flashed across her
mother's face that she didn't want to say. Of course she
wouldn't lie to Rose, so she made no reply.

"Mom, I asked you something."

"A friend," said her mother.

"Was it a fellow asking about Mr. Johnson?"

"He was very charming," said Mom.

"Please tell me who he was. I think I saw him leaving. He went just a few minutes ago, didn't he? Why did he leave in a hurry?"

"He said his name was Croft and that he didn't want to bother me, just ask a few questions. Ever so polite!"

"What did he want?"

He said he was a nephew of Mr. Bernier's." Mom lowered her voice. "You know that Mr. Bernier is not his real name. And I doubt if it's Johnson either. But this young man didn't seem involved in any business. He said his mother, who was Mr. Bernier's sister, was dying and she wanted a photograph of him. And she wanted to hear his voice but you know he doesn't answer the phone to anyone."

"Mom, I don't like the sound of it at all."

"I haven't given him anything."

"Shall I tell Mr. B?"

"The young man said he would appreciate it if we could get him a tape recording of Mr. Bernier's voice."

"Shall I tell the Inspector?"

"What's the need for that? I didn't tell him we'd get him anything."

"It sounds extremely suspicious to me."

"He seems a very sincere young man, Rose."

"We have to tell Mr. B. I don't think this young man is straightforward."

"He asked over and over again about Mr. Bernier's health. He seemed to know all about him. About his head injury and his age and everything."

Rose was furious.

"Mom, you shouldn't talk to people like that. It was you who told me not to say anything to anyone about Mr. B. Did he offer you anything? Like money?"

Rose's mother didn't reply for a moment.

"I didn't take anything from him. At any rate, the old man hasn't once sent me a card or a bunch of flowers in all the time I've been in the hospital."

"He always asks after you."

"That's to get you to work harder. He knows his manners but he's a hard-hearted old devil. I could be dead for all he cares."

"Don't talk such nonsense, Mom," she said, but she thought it was probably true. The old man didn't care about anyone.

"Was this boy about six foot and quite slim? About thirty years old or a little less?"

"I think so. Very handsome."

"Did he say his first name? Or just Croft?"

"Just that," her mother said. "But it's funny how the old man doesn't have any photographs of his family or himself or anyone, isn't it? I've cleaned up for him for years and I've never seen any."

Rose said nothing about the photograph in the pocket of the old fur coat.

When she got to Mr. B's the next day she intended to tell him about this doctor's receptionist who was making enquiries about him. Of course, she would have to tell him that she first met this man the day she went to the doctor's. He would probably ask why she hadn't told him all this before. If it was at all important, he'd be very annoyed.

Rose realized that she didn't even know the old man well enough to know what he would do. She also realized that she was afraid of his possible reaction.

Maybe there wasn't anything to it. Maybe he was telling the truth and was the old man's nephew.

Why was he after a photograph and a tape recording of the old man's voice? The story about sentimental reasons was obviously nonsense, just the sort of thing her mother would fall for.

Rose thought of testing it out. She didn't tell the old man a thing. The next day she took her tape recorder into Mr. B's presence when he was dictating.

"What have you got there, miss?" Mr. B asked.

"A tape recorder."

"Yes, I can see it's not a golf club. Why is it here?"

"I thought maybe I can record what you say and then . . ."

"And then what?"

"And take it home and in the evening or night after the hospital, maybe type it out then."

The old man shook his long index finger in a sweeping motion across his body, like an umpire on a cricket pitch.

"No, sir," he said, "no tape recordings."

"No tape recorder at all?"

"That's what you heard. I don't trust them. Old-fashioned prejudice. You can think that the old man is a bit crazy, but . . . a whim."

Rose put the tape recorder away. It could be, as he said just a whim, or it could be that the old man didn't want his voice leaving the house on tape.

In the afternoon the old man took a bath. While he was in the bath, Rose couldn't resist going to the chest of drawers where his personal papers were and rifling through them to see if there were any photographs. There were all sorts of papers, letters, newspaper cuttings which Rose didn't bother to look at, but no photographs. Not of people, places, nor even of a dog.

Rose looked through the drawers of the desk and in the

pockets of the clothes in the wardrobe. Nothing.

She could hear Mr. B coughing and wheezing at the sink now. She went back to the study. She said nothing to him when he returned wearing a fresh pair of jeans and a checked shirt. Old though he was, he dressed as though he were a teenager. He still had the gaunt body of a tall young man with a flat stomach, no middle-age spread, no balding forehead, all his white hair in a startling thick shock and the only wrinkles round the bottom of his eyes.

He was in a chirpy mood and asked her to run the comb through his wet hair.

"I hate those hair dryer things, I always feel I'll get electrocuted. Where I grew up all you did was walk out in the sun, man, you had a natural hair dryer. Not the women though. As we reached the fifties they had to have perm machines and God knows what from America. You don't have America fever, do you?"

"No, though I do eat McDonald's now and then when I want to save myself and Mom cooking."

"Ah yes, McDonald's. I've seen it on the television. They didn't have it in my day."

Rose didn't know exactly what he was talking about. When was his day? And where?

"You never talk about the Caribbean," Rose said.

"Why pick on that innocent place? I never mentioned the Caribbean."

"Shall I tidy up in the bedroom?"

"The suit could do with a clean. Take it to the cleaners. And take the wretched tape recorder with you."

"Why don't you buy a new one, Mr. Bernier? This one's getting pretty threadbare."

"They don't darn things anymore. I asked your mother to

do this favorite suit which is known as Polly. You know why?"

"No. It's naff calling a suit by name, like a pet."

"I don't understand what naff is," said Mr. B, "but I am a betting man and I'll bet it's rude. I'll tell you it's called Polly because it is pure wool with not a suspicion of polyester or whatever else they put in these suits. It's my grandfather's suit. And you know what I've got against artificial fabric?"

"I don't like plastic cloth myself."

"My dear, no doubt your dislike for artificial fibers owes something to a fine sense of refinement or some aesthetics or art," the old man said playfully, "I have none of these. I am suspicious of these fibers because they ruined the southern economy of the United States, which was based on cotton. The nylon came in and the cotton closed down and the negroes were out of jobs. That gave rise to Martin Luther King and all that civil rights stuff."

"So it was a good thing."

"In a way. It also gave rise to black power."

"How?"

"I think that history lesson is over, my dear Rosey," said the old man abruptly. "Shall we get down to work?"

Rose took the old man's suit, the one he said was his grandfather's, home and in the morning she took it to the shop to be cleaned. The dry cleaner's was just round the corner from her estate and it was run by a Greek Cypriot couple. It was a long narrow shop with machines in the back and a temperature far above that of the outside, a shop with fever. As you approached the counter you passed between two racks of cleaned clothes waiting to be collected.

When she went to retrieve the suit the following day, the proprietor and his wife were both leaning against the counter and two or three people had gathered in the shop to gossip. There were always people from the estate in and out of it and they always swapped stories. There had been a bit of excitement.

"They didn't take anything at all. You see all this customer clothing, all articles we have it insure, but who can say, it's they want cash maybe and maybe not, eh? Villains come and they look in the till and see nothing and maybes they feels too much a nuisance take all the clothes so they just leave everything exact as before and go away." Mr. Karamanlis was excited. It hadn't happened to him before.

Rose gathered that there had been a break in at the shop. Breaking in was a pastime around there. It was never big news.

Mrs. K. volunteered the information that they lost nothing but their faith in the make of lock they had been using.

"Everyone in Cyprus says this lock is best lock, nobody can touch it. But look, they touch it."

"You write to Cyprus and spoil their reputation," said Mr. K.

Rose took the suit in its swaddling of plastic and caught the bus to Mr. Bernier's.

Days later Rose made two discoveries. The old man begged her to fetch mangoes. She said she didn't know where to get them.

"Get them from the Indians or West Indians, or wherever black people live, man, don't you know this town? I miss mangoes, sister. If your mother was in charge she could get me mangoes day or night."

Rose didn't say anything to him but next morning in Brixton market she found a mango. They were out of season and looked hard and raw. If the old devil wanted this kind of mango, well, he could have it.

She took the mango and cut it and presented it to Mr. B who ate it propped up in the leather chair in the study. The juice dripped all over his freshly dry-cleaned suit.

"Come on, get your jacket off," Rose said. "I better put some water on it and get the mark out. Otherwise it will stain."

"Rosey, you're proving a point, aren't you? You're like my second wife."

She never knew he had a second wife or a first one.

He was pulling with his teeth at the mango skin.

"Let's have the jacket, Mr. B," said Rose.

She took the jacket to the bathroom and rubbed at the stain with a soapy flannel.

Then Rose took the jacket, the old blue woolen jacket, property of Grandad Bernier, to the ironing board and began to press it.

In the lining of the jacket, under the pocket there was some sort of intrusion, obtrusion. She felt it. Definitely something. Rose opened the lining with a pair of sharp scissors and found a small electronic packet in a wrapping like scotch tape, with a little bit of wire protruding from it. It had been sewn into the lining.

The raid on the Karamanlis' dry cleaning shop. Herbert? No, why would he want to do that?

Rose eased it out and then stitched up the lining.

Someone has been bugging them. The suit with the device had been back there for several days. What did they want?

Rose decided to say nothing to Mr. B about it. She would have to tell him about Herbert and there was no way she could explain why she had kept quiet about him so far.

Rose found a second microphone.

When she reached the estate and walked up the stairs she felt she was being followed. She turned around but there was no one about. She decided to run to the Ullahs' flat, feeling just a bit silly. She knew there was no one behind her. The footstep was the echo of her own in the stairwell. She got to the top of the stairs, the third floor, frantically searching in her pocket for the key to the Ullahs' flat. She couldn't feel it and didn't want to stop and search her pockets properly. She'd bang at the door, she thought. On the last step she knocked her left heel against the concrete stair and it hung half off her shoe. She was frantic now. She banged as hard as she could at the door and Mrs. Ullah let her in.

"What's the matter, daughter of our house?" she asked in Bengali. Rose didn't understand the language but understood what she was asking.

"My shoe has broken on the stairs," Rose said.

She examined the shoe. The heel had come loose. It hung like a knocked-out boxer's lip. She pulled it off.

It was a curious heel. Hollow inside with a bit of plastic and a little metal piece with holes in its face embedded within. Another device.

Someone wanted to hear what the old man had to say.

They were her day shoes. She only had one other pair. How

did the device get in there? That time she felt someone had broken in? Had she been wearing this pair of shoes or had she left them at home?

She didn't sleep that night. Both the little electronic gizmos were in the kitchen on the table. Rose didn't know anything about electronics, but she'd seen this sort of thing on the television, microphones concealed in odd places. Radio transmitters. Someone at the other end was listening even now.

Rose lay in bed and thought about it. Should she smash them? It would make a racket. She remembered once when she was a child she had gone with her classmates to a camp and they wandered on to a farm where they saw the farmer's wife had caught some rats in a trap and poured boiling water over them to kill them, inviting the kids to watch the execution. The boys talked of it for days afterwards. It had made Rose sick to watch.

The memory came back because that was what she thought of doing now. She'd kill the microphones like rats. She boiled the kettle, put the two tiny plasticky things in the sink and poured boiling water over them. They must have died without a murmur.

The Continuing Story Of Lazarus The Slave

AS TOLD TO SIMON FORMAN

The night after Marlowe left for Paris, Lazarus and I sit and talk as men will who have entered the brotherhood of a secret together. He tells me what had befallen him between my rescuing him and his finding and making a friend of Master Marlowe. Rather, it was the other way around. Kit Marlowe found him.

His own words are best:

I shall always hold myself in debt to you, sir, for saving my life. I left your protection because I could not provide you with the knowledge you were certain that I had. You are a man of great learning and yet with the commonest knave in London you do believe that if a man's skin is black, some magic must be known to him, some devilish art of Africa. The only arts I knew were those that Mr. Walsh had taught me. Chronicles of history and ancient stories, comedies of Mr. Walsh's boyhood days when he went aboard ship to Venice and to Cyprus and to Egypt.

My own travels were my learning. And as I told you, I witnessed many marvelous things myself in my travels through the Indies.

I have observed a yogi drain his blood into an earthen vessel from out a vein and drink it again. And I learnt from them the balances of strength, that a man may lie down and have a tree trunk rolled over him if the weight of the trunk is taken in good measure all over the body.

When I left you and walked into London, still marvelling at the fact that I was alive, I was a creature of the night, afraid to show his face. I sought out that company in which fellow may not betray fellow for fear of being discovered himself. In such low company I spent almost a year, often hungry, always without a roof. It was in this company I came upon one Master Meade who had himself been a seaman and a self-confessed pirate and had sailed to various parts of the continents. He had gathered him in Shoreditch a collection of curiosities and shows, animals and human alike and it was he who on seeing me, gave me employment as a blackamoor. In truth it was an exhibition of great shame, as I was required to go masked but quite naked and with pig's grease upon my body to make it shine and I was exhibited in several postures of lewdness with women of the lowest order, strumpets and whores who were servants of the pirate and adventurer Meade.

It was in this show of the blackamoor and the lady that Master Marlowe discovered me, and lingering after my performance, came to the tent where I was preparing myself for sleep.

"Your heart is not in this business," he said.

At first I suspected him of spying on me as do several men

who go around the city with the purpose of carrying information.

He came accompanied by another man.

"This is the man I want," he said. "He'll play a good devil."

He offered me seven shillings to go with them.

At first I refused his offer and he came back two days later and said he would give me the same money Master Meade paid for a week and then see I got employment regularly in the theater. He said I should go with him and keep him company at a performance of his own play *Tamburlaine*.

In this way I left Meade's show. Master Meade was not well pleased and Christopher had to threaten him with a pistol and strike him on the side of the head before it was resolved that I should be allowed to go.

"Meade does well out of degrading people. Yours is a body that should be admired and placed on an altar."

I was flattered by Christopher's attentions. He would say that he who loves not wine and boys is a fool and he would add that if he had my love and lots of wine he had no need for other boys. I know not what my age is, but I was no boy. I was older than he by my reckoning.

Christopher said to me when I told him my adventures, holding nothing back, "We shall call you Lazarus. You are now given a new life," and he kissed me full on the lips.

I had lain with men before. With men of my tribe in Hispaniola and with Mr. Walsh, and I knew the pleasure of it. And yet Christopher offered a passion that came from the mind. His love had the strength of a conviction, it was a belief and I was the one he believed in.

London was my prison. There was no journeying for me. A

black escaped dog, they would hold me and brand me and bring me back to face assizes and judges. That is all that the fools know. And that is the soul of tyranny, when the people do not know what freedom is.

From The Diary Of Simon Forman

In the year 1594, Lazarus apprenticed himself to Lord Strange's Men and he would in the mornings go down to the Greenwich quay to see certain sailors in the inns there.

He lived in company with Lord Strange's Men and once a week would visit me as a faithful nephew would.

"They will have me on stage when they see a fit part. Mr. Henslowe has given me his word."

"And they keep you in bread?"

"I am something of a shake-scene."

"You move the property on stage?"

"I am, Master Forman, humbled by my needs."

At this time at The Rose in Bankside, Lord Strange's Men perform a play entitled *Titus Andronicus*. This I go to see. Somewhere in the fourth act, this scene being set in Rome, a clown appears with two pigeons in his basket and face painted under his motley. He comes on stage to talk about hanging.

"Ho," he says, "the gibbet maker? He says that he hath taken them down again, for the man must not be hanged till the next week."

I hear these words about hanging and gibbets and I look with keener eyes.

I know the voice. Those lips are unmistakable. Lazarus has ventured out under the cover of a mask.

I wait till the players leave the stage and go to the tent of the players afterwards.

Lazarus greets me.

"What did you think of that play?"

"Your playing was of the best I have seen," I say honestly. "You were the comic who was sad, the melancholy who told the truth."

"This is good of you, Master Forman, but what did you think of the play?"

"It was bloody. Killing for the sport of the groundlings, hack, hack, hack."

He falls silent. We are walking to my house and have now reached my door.

"I do not mean that I did not like it or feel with it. It is a bloody life for sure."

Lazarus freezes and low in his throat there is a high-pitched sound. I had forgotten. On the table in my rooms by the pillar is my victual table and on it this day I had for my science placed the body of a young boy freshly dead in the street. It was unclaimed and the coroner had for a small sum sent it on to me. I had cut the body open and pulled the innards out. Though I had washed it in vinegar and salt water, the body was thick with flies and vermin.

Lazarus gasps again.

"Oh that! I should have told you I am at work on this carcass and the nights being hot, it will begin to smell."

I feel Lazarus slept very little that night, though he slept a chamber and wall away from this unfortunate boy.

The play *Titus* continued at The Rose for several days and each day there would be more clamour amongst the crowd to see this bloody sport. On some nights Lazarus would come after the play to find me and would bring with him one or other player from the company who wanted a meal, or indeed had some ailment and required my physic.

In the marketplaces and on the commons where there were fairs or other gatherings, a man of the company of Lord Strange would herald a message advertising the play. Soon he was no longer required. Men and women flocked to the play. Outside there were furious fights for admittance to the theater as the play began each day. And each day the crowds grew larger and more noisy and the fights and riot spread from the ground of the theater to the river and past The Globe towards the bridge where people took up sides. Some said the play was bewitched and this rumor spread through Southwark and was debated everywhere. The play was, as I have related, bloody and full of hanging and men eating men. Every day there would be shouting and stones would be flung at the stage. Several of the players were injured but Lord Strange's Men kept playing. Lord Derby, whom this company serves, sent word that the play should be called off.

That evening the crowd gathered at The Rose as usual and were told that the play was not to be performed. The crowd broke loose and threatened to burn the playhouse. Lazarus and Master Shakespeare were sent out on horseback to get Lord Derby's express permission to continue the play.

Lazarus told me the story:

We rode to Greenwich and found that Lord Derby had departed. On returning we found a large crowd gathered outside The Rose and Master Henslowe met us.

He was in a sweat. The Lord Mayor had heard of the disturbances in the playhouses and had banned all plays till further notice.

"The order comes too late," he said. "The London mob has filled the theater and their money is taken. They would burn the theater. I beg you to perform, good sirs."

The play proceeded and half the way through at the end of the third act, the Lord Mayor's men were there. They made a proclamation at the door and stood with staves by the stage.

"This play has been performed in defiance of the Lord Mayor's Order and the will of the patron of the players, Lord Derby. It is by the order of the Lord Mayor that the theater is closed and the citizens herein asked to go in peace."

In peace they did not go.

The play being interrupted, the crowd was incensed. They set fire to The Rose and proceeded in procession down towards Lambeth House. The fire was soon put out but in the riot that followed, Master Shakespeare was sorely injured by a stick to his head.

That night Lazarus brought Master S to my lodging and on entry he drew from his waist two bags of coins. They were small silver and pennies. He kept the one and gave the other to me saying he knew I had some need.

"I would not take your money, sir," I said.

"It does not belong rightfully to me but to another who would wish you had it."

"I must know who my benefactor is."

"And I must keep this intelligence from you, nor tell you on what account it was earned. Someone wishes you to have it. For the sake of your physic."

I took Master S in and looked at his head. It bore a gash as deep as an inch in his skull and three inches long, the blood pouring from it. I cleaned the wound with warm water and called Lazarus to hold him while I poured alcohol into the wound. He screamed like a woman who gives birth and swore and blasphemed. He called out to his Maker and put a curse on the House of the Lord Mayor and my Lord Derby and on all who ever went to plays or took the material of plays in such seriousness as to strike an actor with staves.

I poured wine down his throat, too, and in half an hour he slept. On the same bench on which I placed the bodies I cut.

"I must not stay here," said Lazarus, "I have an eye which sees into the events of tonight."

"What fear is there?"

"That Lord Derby's henchmen will be active and they will question me as to who I am. You remember, Master Forman, I am dead. And I have been executed and if I am alive, it is as a runaway pirate."

"Where would you go?"

"I do not know."

"Let's leave the good mummer asleep here. I know a place you can shelter. We shall be a step ahead of them. They won't look in the place they hope to send you."

"What do you mean by the riddle, Master Forman? I am a simple man."

"Mr. W.H.," I said, taking a liberty for once with his name, "that you are not. You shall see and for a few days you shall be the guest of Her Majesty and then return to my humble house."

We walked to the Marshalsea where I demanded entrance. Master Warden would keep Lazarus. Indeed he remembered him and was a man who trusted in miracles. I could see surprise in his face as we walked through the yards and into a chamber, well lit with lamps. Now this warden is a rough man but he stared at Lazarus, and seeing the dead walk in my company, bowed faintly to me and to him and asked how he could be of service.

I gave the dog the bag of coins and said that Lazarus would stay a few more days, in a cell if he must, but not with a chain and in more commodious lodging if the Marshalsea might afford it.

When I returned to my lodging alone, the door had been forced and there was no sign of Master Shakespeare. I thought nothing of it. The most footloose of people in London are those in the acting profession. They know not in which bed they sleep and I doubt if many of them know day from night because they keep no method in when they wake and when they walk.

I was, of course, to see Master Shakespeare again. Two nights later he appeared. He begged lodging and said he had no money to pay but his friends Lazarus and another whom he could not name would give me what I wanted in exchange for any shelter he might have.

"Master Shakespeare, I have never asked you for anything, not even a groat's worth of wit. Where have you been? You look not well-used," I said.

He had a cut beneath his right eye and the hair on his very large and round forehead, a temple of bone, was pulled back and looked torn.

"They treated me as summer and winter treat the earth," he said.

Once an actor always a bloody actor.

"They blew hot and cold upon me. They broke into your lodging and carried me away. They knew me for one of the men who worked in their master's company."

"Derby's men?"

He nodded

"My Lord Derby was annoyed that his order had been disobeyed?"

He shook his head.

"Oh no. I believe Lord Derby was well pleased. He had never known before the power that might come of being the master of a company of actors. You know, Master Forman, that the Lord Mayor had placed a ban some years before and several of our players had been confined by his order."

"So what was he pleased for? And did his men beat you because they were pleased?"

"No. They didn't tell me of his pleasure or displeasure. They took me to a chamber in Eastcheap and kept me lying in a room without water or food or light for I know not how long. Then they entered, three of them, and asked me who had written *Titus Andronicus*. In this cell there was but one stool and they sat me upon it. I denied, Master Forman, all knowledge of who the author might be. I was fearful. They said they must have the name and the man to present to Lord Strange that very day. He would not wait. One of them struck me. I told him that I already was wounded and showed them my head and the lint you placed on it. The one turns to me and says that Lord Strange must be told the truth and was it not I who wrote the play? I said that it was I who wrote it down when the actors spoke their parts, but it was none of my invention. 'If you wrote it, you wrote it,' says the main Jack, and they drag me to a coach in which I am bundled to Westminster into the presence of Lord Strange himself.

"They say, 'This is your man, my Lordship, he has confessed.'"

"I stand there saying nothing till the handsome Lord Strange says, 'Well, I shall have your name sirrah, for never have I seen such passion stirred up by a single play. Most remarkable. You have a rare genius, sir, and I wish to commission you to write for the company a play that can be presented to our gracious liege. Perhaps a play about our heritage. So what was your name?'

"I say, 'William Shakespeare or Warwick, my Lord.'

" 'And you are the one who wrote *Titus Andronicus,* Mr. Shakespeare?' says Lord Strange.

" 'I am, sir,' say I.

" 'Write us then a play more touching on our own times and England. Not too eventful of our time that it may give offence, but not too much in past and in legend that no reflection on us fall from its luster.'

"And before I leave his presence he says, 'I will instruct the Master Burbage and Henslowe that when they advertise your plays by Lord Strange's Men they should add to any advertisement that the play was written or augmented by your good self or others as may write them. Wit must be rewarded and scoundrels with dark purposes must own their deeds.' "

"So you are under commission now to write a play?"

Master Shakespeare said nothing. He sat himself down and I fetched him food and drink.

"I must see our friend Lazarus before the company assembles again beside The Rose tomorrow as we planned."

"You must rest here. Lazarus will appear this very night," I said.

WHAT'S YOUR FAVORITE Shakespeare play?" Mr. B asked Rose.

"I don't know, I don't know them all, so I can't say."

"But of the ones you know? *Romeo and Juliet?*"

"I know that. I did it for GCSE, but I prefer *King Lear*. Did that for A level."

"Why, may I ask?"

"Because it makes you think."

"About what?"

Rose thought she had spent a lot of time with that play. Could she really have a casual conversation about it?

"About everything. The profound things."

"Profound? Which ones?"

"About life and death?"

"Does death interest you?" the old man asked. Rose looked in his face. He was having a serious conversation. He was actually interested in her reply.

"I think it does," she said. "And it scares me."

"It scares you? But you're only eighteen years old or something, aren't you? What scares you?"

"The never, never, never, never aspect of it. That's Shakespeare's phrase in *King Lear*."

"Yes, I know. It doesn't scare me," the old man said. "And you know why?"

"Why?"

"Because I've got nobody. So being dead will be like not having been born."

They didn't say anything more about it. The old man wanted to carry on dictating the story.

The old man had ripped the suit to shreds, the suit in which Rose has discovered the microphone.

The strips lay all over his bed and on the floor. When Rose let herself in, she found him wearing a crumpled old jacket, a thick sweater and jeans with a raincoat on top. It was as though he was twenty years younger. He bounded about fetching papers and throwing them into a suitcase.

"We are going," was all he said.

"Where? Who's going?"

"Listen, can you drive?"

"I don't have a license."

"How do you get about? How can I get about?"

"I go by bus or Tube or walk, or if it's urgent you take a taxi."

"What is that?"

Rose explained.

"Call one of those. There is an envelope in the bottom drawer. It's full of passports. Do you have yours?"

"I got one for the school trip to Florence, but it's a temporary one. It's at home."

"Leave it. I've got enough passports and a stamp or two. Where can one get a photograph of you?"

"At a photo booth I suppose."

"What are they? Why do I ask the obvious? They are booths in which your photograph is taken."

"Automatically, like a slot machine."

"This kind of wonder will never cease. That's why capitalism is still alive."

Rose phoned for a taxi.

"They'll come around in a circle. What do you know of them?"

"Who?"

"The two young men, black fellers who've been sitting in the car in the road opposite. Has someone been following you?"

She looked in his face for any shred of anger. The torn suit had put her on her guard.

"One of them followed me home some days ago and he went to see my mother. He said he was your nephew. I don't know if it's the same person, though. If it is, he used to work at Dr. Trench's. As the receptionist."

He didn't ask why she hadn't mentioned this before.

"Did he mention me?"

"Not you, really, that's why I never told you. He called . . . he wanted somebody called Mr. Johnson."

"Oh my God! He got into Angelina's. I thought I was being careful. I should have known. We got careless. Those damn pills."

"Was it my mistake?"

"No, no, no child. I knew they'd turn up. Now they know where I am. And the microphone. They got a sample of the way I speak. They know it's me."

"What microphone?" Rose asked.

"There it is. In the trousers of the suit you took to get

cleaned. I wore it this morning and felt the weight in the left trouser leg. I tore it open, man. They had sewn the wire right in the hem.''

How stupid of her. Rose could have kicked herself. She hadn't looked in the trousers when she came upon the microphone in the suit jacket. She had assumed that there was only one.

"Why are we afraid of them?"

The old man looked at Rose, noting that she had said "we." He didn't answer her question.

"John . . . what do you call him? The Inspector spotted them and I asked him to cross the road to question them and frighten them off. Of course they'll be back. We have to get away before they come back. Or I can send John out again and then we can get away.''

Rose helped Mr. B down the stairs and carried the small case. They went into the front garden which was cut off from the road by a high hedge. The cab hovered outside and Rose held the old man's hand as he climbed in. The cab was driven by a young black man.

"Where to? Where do you wish to go?'' he asked.

"Just drive off, man.''

"Which direction?''

"Just go to one of the great terminuses, for the north.''

"I don't get that? What you mean terminus, guy?'' asked the man, starting the cab. Rose didn't know either.

Mr. B was obviously not used to being addressed as "guy.''

"A railway station, man. St. Pancras.''

They drove in silence to St. Pancras station, right across town. The traffic was heavy but not stationary. Mr. B wore his wide-brimmed American hat in the cab.

133

Rose wanted to ask him where they were going, but she sensed that this would not be a good idea. She would wait till no one could overhear the reply.

They were dropped off at St. Pancras and Mr. B paid the cab man from a thick wad of notes he pulled out of his inner pocket. The notes had a rubber band around them. There were five and ten and twenty and fifty pound notes.

"How do we get to Birmingham?"

"I think it's Euston station, that's not far."

He anticipated her next question.

"You should phone your mother's ward and leave a message. You'll be gone for a few days but tell her not to tell anyone and say nothing of where you are going."

Rose phoned the ward. The sister on duty, who knew her, took the message.

They caught a black cab to Euston and Mr. B stood by the suitcase while Rose bought the tickets. The train to Birmingham was due to leave in a few minutes.

Mr. B asked her if there was still a first and second class and if there was she was to get first-class tickets.

They ate lunch on the train in the dining car.

The young waitress stared at them. Rose stared back. It was obvious from her eyes that she was making an assessment of this pair. Rose not yet in her twenties, and the old black man with the large-brimmed hat holding on to Rose's arm, unsteady on his feet and fearful of falling. Rose knew that the waitress was waiting for one of them to speak, in order to gauge whether they were Americans or not.

She obliged. They sat at a table for four and Rose said,

"Excuse me, miss, can we have a bottle of mineral water straight away, please?"

She was exaggerating her south London accent. The girl looked dismayed. Perhaps Americans left large tips. She went to fetch the water and a head waiter, a balding fellow, came up and asked them in the politest tones if they were expecting any more people and if they weren't, since the dining car normally got very full on this trip, would they wish to move to one of those tables for two people instead of having other passengers share the one laid for four with them.

"We are quite happy here, old man," replied Mr. B, "I have no fear of strangers, bring them on. No, we shan't move."

"As you please, sir," said the head waiter, though it was obviously not what pleased him. Two blacks refusing to do as he said.

The girl came back and brought them a bottle of water and she was surly. Rose thought the head waiter had had a word with her.

"Can I have plenty of ice?" asked the old man. No "please," no "miss," just the demand.

The girl didn't reply. She gave the old man a filthy look, plonked the unopened bottle of mineral water down on the table and went back to the kitchen. She returned with a plastic glass full of ice and proceeded to put cubes into Mr. B's glass.

"That should cool off the whole thing," said Mr. B. The girl remained sullen. She struggled to unscrew the water bottle. She couldn't do it and Rose said, "here," took it from her and opened it.

"Stiff," said Rose.

The girl grinned and took the bottle to pour it.

"Give it to Julie," she muttered under her breath.

"The name's Rose," said Rose and Mr. B frowned very deeply at her.

"I just said Julie, because, well, nothing . . ."

"Do tell us, young lady, there was a story there. Julie!" said Mr. B.

"Oh, it's nothing. Just we had a girl in school in my class and whenever something impossible turned up, we'd all say, 'give it to her, she'll deal with it.' Like she could bend iron bars or anything."

"You bent a lot of iron bars at school?"

The girl laughed.

The meal was good. The girl leaned over and whispered that if she was them, she wouldn't have the fish. They avoided the fish and chattered with her all through the meal as she served them this and that.

"You think they were ganging up? You think they objected to our color?" said Mr. B.

"I didn't like their attitude at first," Rose said. "They were staring and uptight."

"The British by and large are decent about race. You look odd, they get suspicious, but most of them, there's no viciousness. The English abroad are different."

Rose thought to herself that this might be the opportunity to ask about his experience abroad, but she didn't have to.

"I used to live in the islands. The fellers who came out from Britain to run the administration of the Caribbean, they were full of arrogance, man, and every jumped-up little policeman who was posted there had a little kingdom all his own. We learnt a lot of nastiness from them. But then we had

a lot of nastiness of our own waiting to jump out of the bag.''
He didn't say much more.

The old man had a plan. They were to stay in separate hotels which Rose was to book. If they were followed, the 'boys' would be looking for the pair of them. Rose would find out the names of several hotels and then they would register in them, a few hours apart.

Rose thought of refusing to go at all, but she looked at the desperation on the old man's face. She couldn't abandon him now. It wouldn't do her any harm. Or would it?

He must have read her mind. "They don't want to do us any harm. They want me alive and friendly, I assure you. Treat it as a holiday, but keep your wits about you, we must give them the slip. When I'm settled somewhere you can get back home and I promise I won't forget your assistance.''

The old man produced a bundle of bank notes and put it in Rose's hand.

"Just keep a tight hold of this and of the papers. I entrust them to you. Especially the manuscript I've been dictating. You can use what you like of the money, there's more. Much more.''

The bundle of money contained several thousand pounds. Rose stared at it.

"Don't worry, it's mine,'' the old man said, casually. "You will stay, won't you?''

"I think you'd better keep the money,'' Rose said. "I'll stay. For now.''

From The Journal Of Simon Forman

Since the day Lazarus and Master Shakespeare fled from the riot at the theater, they have been with me. My own chamber is up the stairs so they do not trouble me when they come in of a night.

I have myself been working on the plague and its recurrence here in Southwark. I have noted that those who live closer to the river are more prone to the black death.

Master Will and Lazarus rehearse the lines that Lazarus scribbles. It must be three plays they have worked up in these months.

Lazarus helps Master Will to memorize his lines. Master Will plays Talbot in a new play about King Henry the Sixth. Lazarus will again shift the scenery as there is no part thought appropriate for his talent or his face.

"And whose play is it that must be such a secret?"

Master Will looks at Lazarus, who makes the merest gesture with his eyebrows.

"Why, it is mine, Master Forman," says Mr. Shakespeare.

"I often have difficulty remembering my own spells," I say.

Lazarus shakes his head at me.

The play is so great a success that the company immediately commissions Master Shakespeare to write a second part and even a third. Master Lazarus gets down with quill and candle to compose them each day and night while the drunkard from Warwickshire plays bowls at Newington Butts, drinks at the Mermaid and is now and again entertained by my Lord Essex.

MAY 1595

London has turned unpleasant. There is affliction and sickness everywhere. It is most generally thought that the excessive heat of this summer has affected the air and made the victims easy prey to the dark fluids and perversions of the blood.

I have ministered to members of my own family who caught this pestilence and I have cut their veins before I buried them. On my advice, Masters Will Shakespeare and Lazarus have taken lodgings further inland, away from the pestilent air of the river.

What I know I dare not say in common company, but only amongst men of physic and some knowledge. It is believed that the pestilence visits those whom God sends it to. But prayer is never my answer. All men and women are rogues and none more sinful than the other. This plague does not come from God or the Devil. Air and water carry it and those who catch it must be removed from the company of others.

I have heard this from sailors who have thrown their mates to a watery grave once they caught the pestilence. I journey to Portsmouth at the beginning of the month for I am called by my Lord Monson to find by searching in the charts of the stars where his good ships, which are lost at sea, should be. On getting down to the harbour I hear the cry of a crowd of men. A preacher, later known to me as Liddle, has a group of sailors around him whom he is accusing of the murder of six of their companions who were thrown overboard. Liddle has extracted this knowledge from these sailors themselves who confessed it readily. The captain gave instructions for the affected men to be thrown to the waves. Liddle asks them if it would not be a Christian act to fire on them with muskets or execute them first. The sailors reply that they have not cast these men to their deaths, but thrown them to the care of the sea and of God; and if God has given them the plague, then that is what the Almighty wanted as clear as if He had signed a warrant for their execution.

I am standing at the fringe of the crowd which is being berated by Liddle. In front of me are two men who turn to reveal that they are wearing cowls on their cloaks. As they leave, I have the feeling that one whispers to the other my name. "Forman!"

In the long days of the summer now the Admiral's Men and the Queen's Men perform their last plays as the companies are to close. The governors of the City would burn Southwark and Bankside and call upon their Lord to bring fire and brimstone to the playhouses. The Queen, I am told, is taking the part of the playhouses because the party of the pure gets more and more powerful. They would, if they could, stop all science and learning as well as revelry because just as playing makes a mockery of the one and only Creator, so knowledge makes a fool of His word.

The surprise is that Lord Strange's Men present two new plays, the second and third part of *Henry VI*. I witness them and in my book have the text of the plays. The Constable has sent his men to stand in and around the theaters. They dare not attack the Queen's players till someone at court gives them the signal.

To Blackfriars and the house and printing shop of Master Richard Field. He has sent for me.

"Your friends, Forman," he says, and produces before me two figures, men who stand astride chairs.

They are the same cowls I saw at the meeting in Portsmouth.

"Your friends," he says again, "the figure you most dread to meet. You know them, Master Forman?"

"Not unless they are the angels of death. No, I do not know these."

Their faces are turned away from me and the shadow of their hoods falls deep on their faces.

"You don't know your friends? How will they serve you then?"

"They can serve me by each taking off one glove and showing me their hands. First one, then the other."

"Which one first?" asks Master Field.

I point at the shorter man and a glove comes off. The same long-fingered lily-white hand.

"Then the other hand is black," I say.

The black hand slips out of its glove and grasps my shoulder, firmly, affectionately.

Then they take their hoods off and both Lazarus and Kit Marlowe, as though they had rehearsed it, bow.

"Master Field will publish a humble work of ours, Master Forman, a poem. You must read it and there will be time as we were going to come straight to your house."

"Master Marlowe, why do you make bold to come into London town again? You will be taken and this time you will be hung."

"I tire of France and the French," he says, "and my life is watching other men mouth my words. Also, Master Forman, I begin to miss my friends."

With that he puts his arm around Lazarus's shoulder.

"What shall I call the poem?" asks Master Field.

"It is called by the simplest of names. *The Rape Of Lucrece*."

"And the poet?"

Kit looks at Lazarus.

"It can pay your debts. To whom, my black beauty, do you owe the most money?"

"I haven't been paid these three months and I have had to borrow twenty-nine shilling."

"From whom?"

"From Master Shakespeare."

"Pay the money to him, Richard," says Marlowe, "and write his name on it. Twenty-nine shillings in cash and the rest in reputation. Shakespeare. William Shakespeare. Spell it how you will, it's a plague of a name."

WE HAVE them on the run boys," said Mr. Bernier, even though there were no boys. He sipped his glass of brandy. Rose and he sat in the hotel room they had booked for Mr. B. Her own hotel was a mile away, an altogether humbler affair. It was their first day in Birmingham, but somehow the old man seemed as though he felt safe, as though he felt he had escaped the attention of their pursuers.

"It is a pity," he said to Rose, "that we can't go to the United States. A black man and a lady of your color, no matter what age they were, could lose themselves. I could be the poet and you could be my granddaughter and I would shamble from hotel to hotel on your arm and recite the most exciting poetry. John Donne, Yeats, Eliot, and I could pretend some of it was my own. These Americans wouldn't know the difference. They would reward us handsomely. All you would do is smile and gather the crowds and say, 'Dodo, prove you aren't dead' and then I'd come alive: 'April is the cruelest month, breeding lilacs out of the dead land,' and so on and so forth. We'd make cash man, never go hungry."

He was in high spirits.

"You will have noticed I've changed my mind. Not the brain, just the mind. I shall call myself Longfellow from today on."

He paused for a moment. Then added, "Maybe not, it's a bit conspicuous. Though I've never used it before. But call yourself Smith and they stare at you. Look up something ordinary in the book."

"What book?"

"The bloody telephone directory. You come up with something. The passports in my bag have ten different names on them, but when talking to me we mustn't use those. I've never used Longfellow before."

"What about the Inspector? And the house?"

"Nothing about them. They are gone," said the old man. "And anyway that feller's no Inspector. He's just a paid thug. Private security. The house will stay in the name of Bernier. I'll find a way to transfer it to your mother. She can have it."

"But I've got to go to university or drama school. I'm waiting for my results," Rose said.

"Dear child, you shall go to the best universities in the world, the most sumptuous drama schools. I shall see to that."

"I want to go to the ones I've applied to."

"Of course, of course. How shall we stop you? You've heard of airplanes, flying machines. Marvelous things. Can take you thousands of miles every day, back and forth."

Rose wasn't as sure as Mr. B that they had got clean away.

"Won't the Inspector wonder where you are? He'll ask my mother."

"He has more sense than that. He never knew what exactly he was doing, but he knew enough, and knows enough now not to go shooting his mouth off. I know things he doesn't want me to tell anyone."

"Why are we running away, Mr. Bernier?"

"That won't do at all. Mr. Claude, or just Claude, call me Claude, that'll do handsomely. And I can't tell you till things are settled between us. Now tomorrow you have to go into town and get two tickets from here to Paris and then from Paris on to Toronto. From there we sneak by bus into Buffalo U.S.A. Yippee."

Mr. B, or Mr. C as he now wanted to be called, asked Rose to phone for more brandy because he had drunk the two small bottles in the fridge bar. Rose didn't know what to do. He told her to look at the book next to the phone and dial the number for room service. As she picked up the phone he thought better of it.

"No, no, don't do that, young Rose. They'll get perturbed, they'll get curious, they'll start making enquiries. Leave it, we'll have the champagne instead."

"You needn't drink anything, you know. Why do you drink so much?"

"It's a way of being comfortable with myself. I'll cut down. But tonight," said the old man, his legs stretched before him on the bed, "I must. You know how long it is since I stepped out properly from that wretched house in Forest Hill?" The old man shook his head.

"Where were you before that house?"

"In twenty other such houses. One to the other. There was a time when they were hot on my trail. I thought I'd shaken the bastards off."

"The same people?"

"I have no way of knowing, but give me the champagne. And I know you don't drink but have a sip yourself."

Rose popped the cork and poured it.

"And where were you before all those houses?"

"I was dead, man. Now let's wait for another day. You better get to your own hotel, but phone me, just to say you got there, you know."

"The journey's made me sleepy too," Rose said.

"Will you come for me at seven, we'll call for a breakfast and share it. Then you go and get the tickets."

Rose walked out of the hotel and down the road to her own. Once in bed she lay awake thinking. What was he like when he was a young man? There were no photographs of him except the one in the fur coat. Why?

Rose wondered what the old fellow really felt. If he was living some kind of secret life, there must have been people about whom he had memories. How strange to try and blot out the past, or at least never to allow yourself to speak to anyone about it.

Why the hell had she come with him? What did she think about this old man? She had to admit, he was fascinating, his mind was unlike any other she had met. She had clever teachers, but here was something creative, a writer who had digested a lot of life. And what about the things he didn't say? She now wanted very badly to know who the old man was, whom he had been and what he was playing at. He'd brought her with him because he was going to tell her, surely?

Did he really think she would go to the U.S. with him? He had thousands of pounds in his back pocket. She'd seen the money. Maybe that's what they were after. Perhaps the old man was some big-time Mafia boss or something and these characters were after him for revenge. Rose couldn't remember if they have black guys in the Mafia.

In the morning Rose took a taxi to the Air Canada office and bought the tickets. Mr. B had given her the money in fifty-pound notes and the girl who wrote out her ticket must have been surprised to see this young girl, not particularly well dressed, pulling a wad of money out of her pocket and paying for the tickets in cash, hundreds of pounds.

Rose had her passport photo taken in a booth and returned to Mr. B's hotel to explain that she couldn't get any tickets via Paris and then on to Canada for the next day, but that they would have to stay over for a couple of days before a booking from Birmingham was available.

She looked around the town and spent some of the old man's money on a new jacket. In the afternoon she went back to her room and later she phoned Mr. B and went over to the hotel.

The old man was glum about the prospect of staying longer and he grumbled a bit but then cheered up when he got Rose to order dinner in the room and call for some more champagne.

"Let me get on with my story. Remember I said I was dead?" Mr. B asked. "Well, I wasn't fooling about, I was proclaimed dead. I won't tell you just how and why, but man, I have seen some awful things and been treated in some awful ways. These fellers, brutes, formerly my friends, my companions, they strapped me to a bed with a woman who was my friend and they were going to kill. I was no young man, I couldn't have got anywhere, and three times they gave the order to kill me. The sons of bitches.

"And they would tell some feller, 'go kill the old man' or 'old Shaky' — from Shakespeare, you know — and the young boys who were supposed to carry this killing out, they didn't want me dead. I used to teach these fellows and their fathers when they were in school. I was known in the whole country for the finest style of teaching Shakespeare ever. Better than all the Englishmen they had had right down the years in the school. So they knew me and there was no way they were going to shoot me, just because some cock-eyed bastard said to go kill him.

"The point is, my dear Rosey, the last lot of soldiers who were guarding me and let me go, they went through my house with a fine-tooth comb. They knew me, my affairs, what I'd done for the government, what I thought against it, my diaries, my personal letters, everything. They know me well and now . . . maybe they are looking for us."

"You mean looking for you? Why would they be?"

"They know I am alive. Or they suspect."

"But you are alive!"

"I'm rambling, man, rambling. Forget it. Think nothing of it."

"That wasn't rambling, you were telling a story. Why did they tie you to the bed? Where are we talking about?"

"We shall start all that tomorrow, Rosey, but for now, let me tell you about the work you are doing with me. If this is impertinent, please tell me. You understand what I mean by 'impertinent'?"

"Yeah, yeah. We call it 'out of order,'" Rose said. She sensed that he was vaguely embarrassed by having to talk this way.

"Yes, 'out of order' — good phrase. I hope I am not being out of order, but the truth is, I don't just want you to work for me, I want to adopt you. I know all about your father disappearing and never coming back. I didn't know the feller, but I know the type. Now I've brought you into all this because I feel responsible for you. I have no children, no relatives and I have some little money stashed away. Before you say anything, I know we shall have to talk to your mother. As soon as we get loose of these characters who are following us, we shall do just that."

Rose was stunned. What could she say?

"You see," the old man said, "the last time we talked about death and all that it was about *King Lear*. Do you remember? I said I wasn't scared and all this. Well, it was a lie. Or a partial lie at any rate. Now sit back and let me tell you something."

Rose sat back.

"This story I'm dictating to you, dear girl, it's a true story. I haven't made it up. First, I've got to finish it. Second, you have to defend it when they come for me, when they come at me after I'm dead and say this is all a pack of lies."

Rose stared at the old man and then looked away.

His voice changed. "Was that out of order? Are you offended?"

"Of course I'm not offended. But why me?"

"Who else? You are my friend. I know the family. You are a black girl. You've helped me. I want to feel I've done all this for somebody, for something. I shall die soon, or maybe not so soon, but then what'll happen to it all? The books, the money?"

"Yes, okay," said Rose. She didn't know quite what she was saying yes to.

"Then you'll be my daughter, you see."

"That's right Mr. B, but I don't think I know you well enough for that. Not yet. Who are these people chasing you?

Why are you running from them?"

"I can explain all that. Tomorrow?"

Rose nodded.

The next morning Rose went to the old man's room. He didn't allude to their conversation of the previous night but said instead that they must get on with the dictation. They worked all day in the room.

Around eight o'clock Rose went for a walk and when she came back she found the old man already dressed for bed.

"Your bedtime story," he said, "the one you asked for last night."

They ordered a brandy for the old man and when it came, he began.

"A small West Indian island. Clump of dirt in the Caribbean. That's where I was born. I came here and studied and went back with my head loaded with ideas like a bomb. I was going to change the world. The world had its own ideas. So I went to the U.S. and wrote books instead. I wrote a lot of books. Novels. Politics, telling people why this was happening in the Caribbean, in Africa, in Europe, in the United States, why this was happening and not that. Some explanation. A scheme of the world. And once you write like that, you know, people read it and they believe you can run the world better. And what's worse, you believe it too.

"You may have read yourself the lessons of history. Those who write history rarely make it. Those who describe societies rarely govern them. Sometimes they do. Lenin and Hitler. In the West Indies and Africa, some. They start by describing and prescribing and people think they're clever and then put them in power. I got tied up with one such gang. They thought I could run their revolution so they called me back from the States. I was happy there, man. Quite content, you know, giving my lectures and fighting the world's revolutions from my platform.

"They sent for me. They had seized power in this tinpot place. With guns. I had been talking about guns for years. These guys had them. The army was a hundred fellows in singlets and khaki pants and old rifles. They just walked in and they called me. I went.

"I told them, one, that I was happy to be home and accept the job of running their information machine. And two, I said you must stop talking nonsense because this place here doesn't have nothing. We have a few spices and we grow a few bananas. That's it. No oil, no bauxite, no uranium, no nothing. Stop talking all this bullshit about socialism. You can't have banana socialism. For that you need money, factories, something more than what we got. We can give the people good and clean government, that's all. That's what I am for. Good government.

"That's what I said and one of the fellers in the leadership, the prime minister, he liked all that good sense and he said yes, that's what we'll give these people, a good government and some teachers for the school, roads, hospitals, a chance to buy and sell and carry on all manner of cultural activity freely . . .

"The other fellow, a little stocky with bulging eyes and a vicious petty mind, he just glared at me. He had dreams of what he called waking up the whole of the Caribbean to revolution. To set it on fire. Of course, under his able leadership.

"These small fellows get big dreams and they're always the boss in them. He wanted to put out vast worldwide propaganda saying that our island was another Cuba and so on and that the Americans were demons. I said they were rich demons and we should get some money from them on our own terms so we had to play carefully.

"They made a mistake. A deep mistake. They gave me the newspaper to run. A small affair. A few thousand printed every two days.

"Elections. I started calling in the paper for elections. The first time I wrote about the possibility of having more than one party, young Bullfrog summoned me to his office. He attacked me.

"What do you think you're doing, you old goat?"

" 'I sit in that newspaper office and I hear a thousand stories. People come to me with them. They don't go to you because all you want is business and flattery. Things are going on with our party that you don't realize. Corruption, extortion, filth of all sorts, favors of all sorts. People are muttering. Even amongst that little boy-scout troop you call an army. The only way is to call the opinions out. Out of the closet. Stand for election, take your care to the people.'

"Bullfrog just listened that day, he said nothing. The prime minister was my friend. We used to talk and as soon as he heard I'd been summoned to Bullfrog's presence, he called and drove his Jeep around.

" 'What did he want?'

" 'What we expected.'

" 'And now?'

" 'Keep at it. More articles.'

"It lasted two and a half years and then they fought. I could see it coming from the beginning. They fought and the Bullfrog's men came for me.

"They shot the prime minister and they killed the half of the government who they thought might stand in the way of them taking over and they sent to put me in prison. There were that day too many people in prison so they sent me for 'debriefing' to a house on the hill with three soldiers and they tied me to the bed and they tortured me. They wanted to know some things I didn't want to tell them. I said I knew nothing. They had jailed half the army who then broke out of jail after two days of this and fought for Führer Bullfrog and restored some sort of government and invited me to stay. But, boy, I'd had enough.

"You know what the sons of bitches did? They declared themselves a military government of 'the revolution.' They didn't see it was funny. They had learnt these words. Bullfrog had taught them a few words. They were throwing them around. They said to me, 'Comrade, you will give evidence at the trial of the reactionary criminal clique.' I had nothing against seeing those murderers hung, but not by this lot. I got out, man, I got out."

The old man paused. There was no emotion in his voice at all as he told the story. The story may not have been told before, but it had been rehearsed a thousand times in his head.

"So that is it, Rosey, and it's best I avoid seeing my old friends. They want to kill me and now, dear Rose, they want to kill you too."

"Kill me for what? What have I got to do with it?"

"You've tied yourself up. I didn't suggest you leave with me just for fun. I think there's some danger."

"But kill you for what? Because you didn't go to the trial or support them? I don't get it, though, who's trying to kill you?"

"That's part one of the story. Just go carefully and carry a big stick. You know Rosey, I don't like us staying three days. We should check out of this town and go to Shakespeare's birthplace. Not that the drunken man from Warwickshire matters to me, but it'll get us away from Birmingham till we wait for the plane."

"They couldn't get us a flight any earlier."

The old man waved her away. He was falling asleep.

"Tomorrow, order us a cab to Stratford, check out of your hotel and I'll check out and we'll find a small hotel there. Before we set out, go to the bookshop and buy me these three books."

He handed Rose a piece of paper on which he had scribbled the titles and authors of the books he wanted. One was a long poem by a Caribbean writer, a book which had been much reviewed in the papers. The old man had torn the reviews out and kept them. The second was a novel by an Indian-sounding bloke and the third was a travel book by a famous West Indian writer.

"I hope you'll get them in this godforsaken place."

From The Diary Of Simon Forman

(1595)

A woman comes to me in the chamber above the taproom of the Cardinal Wolsey ale house. They are all after me now, cousins, clients, noblemen and whores. The landlord knows that he can share in this bounty and allows me the room upstairs for consultations. I cast figures from the stars and answer the clients' questions.

Today, there comes a fat woman, the last client. It has been market day in Deptford. She wears silks and a heavy wool scarf. It's a hot day and she must be uncomfortable so I ask her to set her scarf down and open the window if she wants air.

"I shall not go to the window. I do not wish to be seen," she says. She tells me she is a merchant's wife and he has newly returned from the East. She had been the owner of jewelry and a score of bracelets, that is till the day before.

"They were stolen from the inn in Deptford where I had the misfortune to spend the night."

"One belonging to Mistress Eleanor Bull?"

"Yes. The very same. They were taken from me while I slept."

Had she reported the theft?

"Yes, to the sheriff, but the shrew Mistress Bull said she saw no jewelry on me when I went to my room."

Of course she wants me to find, by whatever magic I can, who has stolen her jewels.

I cast the figures from her day of birth, which I suspect she lies about.

"I see in all this a dark man," I say.

"Dark of hair or of skin?" she asks.

"My lady, I meant one with dark hair."

"My husband is of dusky hue," she says, "he was born in Lebanon and is yet a Christian gentleman."

She would have chattered on but I say that I am convinced that this dark man of Lebanon was himself the thief.

"The thief? My husband steal the jewels he gave me himself?"

"Was he near by?"

"Why, he was at my side!"

"And remained there all night?"

But I can see she blushes so I raise my hand to show I need no answer.

"He came to bed later and rose earlier. We have been travelling. It was Mistress Bull that suggested you and your figures to me and it is my husband who shall pay you for your pains. He, too, would know where these stones and gold went."

"Did you or your husband see another dark man on your journeys during the day?"

"For myself I cannot say I did, but my husband went into

Mistress Bull's house earlier for a drink. It is a house where gentlemen repair."

"I know the house," I say, "you must ask your husband."

And with this I leave her, asking her to return in a day or two.

I make my way home and find there Masters M and L. They are the worst for drink, though Lazarus when drunk is full of talk and Master Marlowe given to smiling and smiling and only sharing as much of his wisdom as would make one thirsty for more. Lazarus excuses himself for invading my home and says they must stay in town tonight and they put forth a purse of money straight-aways and Master Marlowe says:

"I would love to be invited to be your guest, Master F, and we won't be in your way as you are out by day and we are out at night. How do you astrologers say it? Like as two planets of the same sphere that never meet?"

"Well done, Master Marlowe. You are of course welcome." Lazarus says, "Celebrate."

"Your homecoming?" I ask, taking the flask he proffers.

"That and the new play by William Shakespeare. A true tragedy."

My eye falls upon the table where next to a jar that Lazarus has been using is a pile of jewelry, jade and amethyst and gold.

There was no mistaking it. The description of it was fresh in my mind and I had formed a clear picture of these baubles as I had to make the effort to see them from her words. The jewels of the Lebanese merchant's wife.

"So you've been buying each other necklaces from the proceeds of your tragedy?"

"The proceeds of the tragedy have, tragically for us, proceeded to Stratford in the pocket of our friend Master Will who demands more and more of a share as the plays and days proceed."

I am in no way surprised that Lazarus, after all his acquaintance with the world of actors and stages and the people who traffic around them, has turned to the buying and selling of thieves' property. He has had no way of earning for a time now and suddenly Master Marlowe returns, I would swear, without a penny with which to entertain himself.

"So whence came you by this treasure?"

"From a tomb," says Master Marlowe. "The kings of Babylon were buried with their treasures so they could return and use them."

"Did you perchance return them, Master Marlowe, to a certain house in Deptford?"

"How did you know that?" asks Lazarus.

I bow.

"This fellow hears things round and about."

"And perchance you had them from a gentleman who, like the wise men following a star, comes to London from the cedared country of Lebanon."

"Damn this fellow! How have you found this out?"

Master Marlowe is unmoved by my revelation.

"Lazarus, we have seen something stranger than Master Forman's intelligence. We met today, Master Forman, with a man whom I know from Paris. And you are right, we did visit Mistress Bull. I met a man there I knew from Paris. He is here to see his wife. He gives her jewels and then steals them to sell and pay back the loan with which he bought them."

"And not knowing London, he has given them to us to

sell. Now he will have to find, not a buyer but the pair of us who have his jewels,'' says Lazarus.

"So you have turned common thief?" I ask.

"I shall be forced to challenge you to a duel, Master Forman. Unless of course you pass me the flask of wine."

So we drink and then sleep.

This tragedy of Master Marlowe's was *Richard II* and it tells the sad story of the deposition and imprisonment and death of the King and of the force of arms used against him by Bolingbroke of Lancaster.

The play was a bold stroke, for never before had the apprentices of Southwark seen a king replaced not by his son, but by another who wins a throne with a sword. I said this to Master Marlowe who was much at home and spent his day sending for notes and books through Lazarus and scribbling his folios in his room.

"In Edward we killed a prince, but then his son took the throne. This play brings alive the rewards of weakness and corruption. The King allows weeds to choke his garden. And what do we see today in Protestants and Papists alike? Flatterers all."

"So the play has a lesson?"

"Not one that will be easily learnt."

"Does one see plays for learning?"

"Plays bring back the past because nothing else can. For the rest the world is also a stage."

I was not the only one who remarked that there was a dangerous lesson in *Richard II*, though at its first playing it was poorly attended and not much talked about. The Chamberlain's Men presented it a few times but tired of it. One of Lord Essex's men attended one of the performances. Lazarus came home one day to report that Henry Wriothesley, Earl of Southampton and friend of Essex had been in person to see Master William Shakespeare, whom he had been told had devised the play.

He had paid Master Will handsomely, "for the enjoyment of the play," he said, and had given him invitations.

Master Marlowe was much amused.

"Master Shakespeare, off the stage, plays a very clever game. He keeps his mouth shut, except opening a chink in it now and again to smile. He gives the appearance of thinking deeply and saying little so as to keep his talents together. The truth, of course, is Master Shakespeare has no lines to speak until we write a part for him and feed him speeches. But men think him wise. They listen to their own voices and he merely smiled."

Soon after that conversation, Lazarus returned from the playhouse to say that William Shakespeare had been detained by two men who came from the Knight Marshall's office. They wanted to question Master Shakespeare about a plot. Why had he written this play? Who had paid him to put this on the London stage?

"If that stiff icicle of an actor melts, they will come for you. All sorts of rumors are about," I say.

"He won't melt. He has played the game too far. And anyway, he knows nothing of me. Only that you deliver lines and scenes and these one by one so that spies from the Admiral's may not get the whole play."

The next day and the day after, the Knight Marshall's men returned to the theaters. Master Shakespeare did not reappear and this gave Lazarus some pause.

"You must go and I'll go with you."

"To France? As my slave? You will have to pretend you are dumb. A blackamoor who speaks English will be taken for a runaway or a renegade and questioned and sold again. No, my dear, you remain and I shall be back. You should locate Master Will."

The next day Marlowe was gone.

A week after that, Master Shakespeare turned up and had words with Lazarus. He was wearing a cape with the Southampton arms on it and had a man-servant who waited on him.

"They held me for three days and I admitted that it was all my work and no one had conspired with me. They said they had taken note of me and wanted to know what I was going to write next and if it was full of treason."

"And how did you answer?"

"I didn't know how to answer. I remembered that Kit spoke of a Roman tragedy of some sort and that's what I said. Now they wish to see it. Do you have the play?"

"Will, Kit had to flee. We didn't know what you'd tell the Knight Marshall."

"But you have the play? They want it. And Essex and Southampton, to whom I've boasted this warlike Roman tragedy."

"I have something of it, Master S. I am sorry, it has but three acts."

"Then you must finish it. You know his mind. You have studied these matters."

"It is again about the death of tyrants. Julius Caesar is stabbed by conspirators and Antony avenges him."

"Mr. Walsh gave you some learning in these things, did he not? In the Latin and the Greek?"

By the morning, Lazarus had written the last two acts of the play and that evening, having slept not at all, departed for the theater.

"If Master Shakejaw has no play to show them, they will begin to suspect and question and seek," said Lazarus.

When the Chamberlain's Men played at the theater I went to see this *Tragedie of Julius Caesar*. A broken-backed play it was, a tied-together thing of two separate plays. Of course none knew what I knew, that the men who made it were two separate beings, one of passion for the first part and one of enduring, both of learning, one born to it and the other brought to it by the grace of God and the favor of a ship's captain called Walsh.

Over a year has passed since Master M left for Paris. And no word.

Lazarus is not a happy man. He sits of a night after performances, in which he plays some part of an attendant or one who holds a spear, and he writes long letters which he goes down to the docks to hand to sailors, with commissions to take them to France to Monsieur Christophe. Never have I seen a man more stricken for the love of another, though I have seen fathers and mothers bring their sons and heirs to me to buy potions to make them love women and to leave their longing for the body of a man. There is no such potion, not one whose effect does not dull the spirit.

I tell him that Master M will no doubt return. The Admiral's Men are even now preparing to mount the plays which go under his name, *Tamburlaine* and *Doctor Faustus*. I tell

Lazarus that Master Marlowe's one great failing is vanity and he will want to see the effect that these performances have on the crowds.

"Some misfortune may have detained him."

"Master Marlowe? Misfortune? He frightens fortune and misfortune alike. Even if he's in Hell he will turn up to see his own plays and watch the fickle mob applaud."

Lazarus does not agree.

In the last year there has been but one communication from Marlowe. This note he sends in the hands of a sailor who says he comes from Spain. With the note is a pack of two plays.

Lazarus ponders over this note for weeks. He reads it over and over again.

"This may buy your bread" is all the note says.

It is not signed.

In the last year Lazarus has written two plays and given them for performance under William Shakespeare's name. They are *The Comedy Of Errors* and *Two Gentlemen of Verona*, both merry plays to ward away the devils of his own longings.

Master Shakespeare pretends to share the invention of the story with Lazarus and spends days with him while he composes, adding nothing but a chuckle here and a long bombastic reading there. He reads the speeches and scenes pompously to see if the plays satisfy his reputation. For my part, I think this William Shakespeare quite content with any piece of rhyme after a few glasses of wine, especially if he is given lines to read. I have observed that it is ever thus with actors.

The playwright Greene on his deathbed penned something to offend Master Shakespeare. He called him "Shake-scene" and "an upstart crow." It amuses Lazarus till I tell him that the writer of the remark died in his own vomit, poisoned by pickled herrings, a penniless wretch, famous for an hour or two for the plays he wrote and then cast off to be heard no more.

He confesses that he is being pursued now by the Lebanese merchant and his friends, who thirst for his blood. He took their jewels to sell and lived off the proceeds. He must go carefully if he goes at all in the streets of Southwark.

One day Lazarus returns from the theater and tells me of a young man, one Sebastian by name, who has arrived at The Rose with a note for Master James Burbage and a new tragedy which Burbage is much taken by. He has just returned from foreign lands and has brought this play on the condition that he can play in the role of the star-crossed lover, the girl who is loved by a youth of Verona.

Burbage calls Master Shakespeare and asks if this is any of his work.

"Verona? Are all poets taken by Verona? This would be in your hand and seems of your style."

Master Shakespeare has never heard the story of Romeo and Juliet, but that would never stop him accepting any credit that may come to him for it. He only smiles.

Lazarus begs to see this marvel script and he brings it home and pores over it all night. He is satisfied and he looks as pale as a black man can, as if the plague had him.

"It is in his hand, and Master Simon I know him, it is a story of the death of lovers and I can see Christopher laughing as he writes it."

The young man Sebastian plays Juliet when the play opens at The Globe. The next day Lazarus disappears.

ROSE ASKED at the hotel desk. There are a few bookshops, what would she be looking for?

"Novels?" the man asked, "Magazines? We have some in the shop in the arcade."

"Poetry, literary criticism, that sort of thing."

"I see madam," he said and suggested a shop in town.

The shop was huge, on several levels, divided in two by an arcade corridor.

Two of the books the old man wanted were there. As Rose paid and left she spotted a young black man in a red wool cap looking at her. He moved away around the corner at a brisk pace. Rose stood in the one way street and waited for a cab. Before one arrived, dashing around the corner with the boy in the wool cap came Herbert, Mr. Receptionist Herbert.

Rose's heart pounded. So they'd found her and the old man.

"Hello, we thought we'd never find you. We were going to give it a few more days, Thank God."

He sounded gentle, as though he had known her all their lives, like a big brother, concerned for a sister he'd lost.

"Rose child, you gave us a fright."

He motioned the boy in the wool cap away. The boy turned around and disappeared.

Herbert didn't touch Rose, but he went on quietly, inviting her to walk with him.

"We shouldn't make a scene of course, we'll just go and have a coffee and talk, shall we, Rose?"

"How did you find me?"

"Bookshop. Mr. Johnson should really learn to live without books."

"How did you know it was Birmingham?"

"We have men in every town with a major airport. Yesterday I was in Glasgow and then Edinburgh the day before and you just walked into my arms today. Look, we don't want to harm the old man, we want maybe to talk to him. Unless talking to you will do, then he can go where he likes."

They came to the doorway of an old hotel and Herbert paused in the manner of a Victorian gentleman, holding a door, almost bowing.

Rose turned into the lobby. Herbert knew where the lounge was.

"I didn't say the old man was here, I mean in town. He's gone already."

"No, he hasn't Rose."

"What makes you think I'll tell you anything?"

"Rose, we've waited such a long time. We want to share something with you."

"Who's this 'we' you keep talking about?"

"My friends. No, correction, my associates. They are not nice people. They'll kill someone for what they're after. Not me, I don't do them things."

"I can't help you, really. I know nothing about the old man. Mr. Johnson."

"I'm going to let you go back after this chat to wherever he is. Nothing will happen to you. But I want to ask a few questions."

Rose said nothing.

"Well, Rose, you know, I know what you're up to."

Rose made no answer.

Herbert began to recite:

"The parting fancy of a player's speech
Before the night on thrifty tones doth fall
And each as witness turns an ear to each
'Fore darkness covers watchers, shades and all . . .

"You see I was there before you."

"At the church in the East End?"

"What church?"

"No church. Where were you before me?"

"It's no great mystery, Rose. I was taking dictation from the old man, transcribing his manuscript, this Simon Forman diary long before you."

Rose stared at him.

Was this a bluff to extract information from her? How would he have known about the diary anyway? She hadn't even told her mother what she was doing for the old man. She had said she was writing something with him, but not the content.

"My mother has been with him for several years, she didn't say anything about you."

"Your mother? Long before your mother, Rose, ages before. When I was maybe your age. Not here."

"If you wrote it down yourself, then what do you want from me?"

"Ah, we never finished it. That was a story interrupted by revolution and suicide and death and my suspicion that he wasn't dead at all."

"I don't know what you're talking about."

"I'll tell you. You tell me the rest of the story. You see, I think there's a clue or two in it."

"As far as I can see it's just a diary which Mr. Claude's got hold of."

"Mr. Claude? Wonderful. And Mr. Longfellow? and Mr. Johnson? He's a great writer of stories. He used to teach my father when he was a boy."

"Good, but there's nothing I can tell you."

"Where's the diary? Finished?"

"I don't think so." That might buy more time.

"Really? Oh, oh. That's one misjudgment on my part. I thought you'd have a copy and would go to the public library to get a photocopy. Or maybe not. You'd go to the High Street copy shops."

"Well, it isn't finished."

"But you can show me what's done, can't you?"

"Why should I? Can I go now?"

"No, please. Just talk to me."

"About what?"

"The old man. Has he told you any other stories?"

"No, I do the cooking and cleaning. I take things to the dry cleaners. I spend my time looking for hidden microphones. No time for stories."

Herbert smiled. "Good, very good. What did he say about the Caribbean?"

"Nothing about the Caribbean. I never even knew he had any connection with the West Indies."

"Connection? He was born there and he died there."

"Died?"

"Yes, committed suicide. Walked into the sea. Left his clothes on the beach. He went back to America. He must have had a small boat waiting with some clothes. The small boat took him to a larger one, I suppose."

"I don't know anything about that. I want to go."

"No, I think you'd better wait. Don't you know how we found that he was alive?"

Rose didn't answer.

"Vanity, man, these writers have vanity. They can't stop. The idiot goes and publishes a short story in a literary magazine and calls himself Johnson. One of our men came across it. Unmistakable style, though he had moved on. Couldn't keep quiet. He had millions. Millions of dollars. He doesn't need the money."

"What millions?"

"Maybe you can tell us, Rose. They're not his. They belong to the legitimate elected government now. Only they don't know it and what they don't know can't excite them or hurt them."

"Which island?"

"You've heard of it. Santa Bella. Yes, the place the Yankees invaded."

"And you're from there?"

"From London mostly. But when the revolution broke out, I was hanging around picking pockets and smoking ganja. It was my baptism of fire. I went 'back home' to my father's island and joined the new revolutionary guard army. Playing at soldiers. Only they gave us real machine guns and Jeeps to drive."

"And you want this money for yourself. You mean fuck the legitimate government, you want to get your own dirty hands on it."

Herbert looked at his hands as though to ascertain whether they were dirty. "I'll show you something."

He delved in his pocket and took out a photocopy of a poem. He handed it to Rose.

"What do you suppose that is?"

"It's a sonnet."

"Very good, read it to me. Keep your voice down."

Rose read it:

> " 'No lover grieves when I embrace the wave
> No dark of mourning falls on anyone
> I leave this verse to grace an empty grave
> A reference point to say "A life is done."
> "That was his name, his dates, make use of those
> To piece together a picture which can tell
> You more about him than the poems or prose
> He left behind. Of all the souls in hell
> (The numbers grow) he rises from the deep
> Ocean, washed, not all his conscience clear
> The mote that irritates the eye of sleep."
> That's all I'll say before I disappear.
> No. One last thing, let silences be heard
> On my account let no man speak a word.' "

"So what do you think?" Herbert asked.

"I don't think anything."

"I would really appreciate it if you did think."

"What do you mean?"

"Let's be straight, right? The old man left this poem

for me. It's his epitaph. To be written up on his tombstone. He left if for me to work out. But I think he's changed his mind. I think he's going to give you a copy. Or maybe not. Maybe he'll just tell you where the money is and how to get to it."

"Why should he do that?"

"He has no one else. You become his heiress."

"How do you know he was going to leave the money to you?"

"He wasn't. He said he was going to share it with me for letting him escape. He was minister in the government that was axed and I was guarding the old man. He told me he had cash stashed away and he hinted it was in an account. It could only have been in Switzerland. He'd pay me for letting him get away.

"I couldn't fix his escape, there were others and there was nowhere to go from that island. He used to talk to me. He started this diary business. We grew quite close, you know. He used to say if he got to the States or England he'd call me over and he was hinting he'd treat me like I was family or something.

"Then the bloody Americans invaded and started throwing grenades and shooting up everything. In the confusion I lost the old man. We were rounded up by the Marines. The old man was a big hero again. Except of course he had the money and no one else knew, except me and the other brothers who were guarding him. So he planned a little suicide. He left the poem as a suicide note together with instructions for his burial."

Rose read the sonnet again. "I don't even know what it means."

"The Americans, Russians, Cubans, all sorts of people

gave Santa Bella some heavy aid. For education. The old man salted it away. I believe somehow, between you and me, we can get at the numbers of the Swiss bank account. They are somewhere in this poem."

"Numbers?"

"Yeah. Which numbers though?"

"He didn't tell me anything. Look, I'm paid to keep him fed and clean and take notes, I told you."

"Does the sonnet mean anything to you?"

"Nothing at all."

"He left instructions with it. The idiots in the new government actually made a little monument for him."

"How do you know it's not just a sonnet?"

"Because the old man used to read these things with me and he used to say, 'There's no such thing as just a sonnet. The Elizabethans put their secrets in poetry.' "

Herbert leaned across and gripped Rose's wrist.

"I'm not supposed to say this at all, but you solve this and it'll be between you and me. You're really fit, you know sister? Anyone tell you that shit?"

Rose was amazed. Suddenly Herbert had turned from this shadowy Mafia sort of person to the black boy at the blues asking for a dance. He grinned.

"C'mon, sister, you're cool too, you know. You crack this with me and we could inherit, not the earth but a sweet, sweet slice of it."

"You mean get together and rob the old man?"

"Rob what? Rob nothing, gel. It's not his money and he wants to leave it to you and he did once promise it to me. So okay, we're taking him up on it. Not even all of it. How much does he need to live in any style he wants? A few hundred thousand? Great. We'll give him a chunk, share it out if he signs a will saying we get it after he dies. I mean really dies this time. But of course he doesn't want to do any of that because he's pretending he's already dead."

Herbert was searching her face to see if she understood.

"And he's afraid that since he doesn't officially exist anymore, anyone can kill him."

"You got it! Tell me Rosey, what's his memory like?"

"Pretty good."

"Sure? Can he remember phone numbers, for instance?"

"Maybe not. He asks me to look them up."

"See what I mean? But he can set himself little mazes and puzzles and remember the number that way."

"Why was he making you write down the story? On Santa Bella, I mean? Why not write it himself?"

"Partly to keep us amused. Partly because he's so vain he can't exist without teaching people things and we were his only audience for those months. Partly because his hand shakes. Can't write or type and he doesn't trust tapes."

Rose nodded.

"And we give what you want to your mother."

"Very neat, mister, but I know as much about the mystery numbers as you do. Which is nothing."

"What's all this 'mister,' Rose? Maybe I forgot to introduce myself. I'm Herbert, man. Call me Herbie. They used to call me Herbie, but not for short, you know."

"You tied him to a bed and beat him."

"Ah, so you were lying. He has told you about Santa Bella."

"And you were lying. You weren't passing the time taking notes, you were torturing the old man."

"That's bullshit. No one touched him. He just likes to make himself a real sufferer with torture and crap."

Herbert kissed his teeth in contempt. "We made him food and everything. Tied him to what? He was free in the house. He even had a girlfriend, the dirty old man."

"And they took other people out and shot them?"

"Yeah. They did shoot plenty of people. But they got hung too. I left man, I came back to London."

"Look Herbert, suppose there are no numbers, suppose it's all a wild goose chase?"

"There are two words in the last two lines. It can't be a coincidence."

Rose looked.

The last two lines. "No. One last thing let silence be heard/On my account let no man speak a word."

"There are lots of words," Rose said.

"The two I'm thinking of are 'Account' and 'No' with the full stop on. Meaning Account Number."

Rose looked again. Now that he'd mentioned it, the two words stood out.

"Somewhere in those lines is the complete clue. I've lived with this bloody thing for years. You have a go."

Herbert handed her a copy of the old man's epitaph.

"Why don't I just ask him straight?"

"Why don't you. What do you think he'll say?"

"He'll think I've joined your gang or was part of it from the start."

"Right. He'll never tell you."

"What about the rest of your gang?"

"You'll have to leave them to me. Just find out the end of the diary. In some way, Lazarus and Master Forman are going to give us a clue."

"Perhaps they already have," said Rose. "The same sonnet with two different endings. One I suppose for Kit Marlowe and the other — of course. For Lazarus."

"I didn't even get that far," said Herbert.

"Do you think Lazarus is buried in that churchyard in the East End?"

"Could be. But it doesn't get us closer to the number."

"That's not all that's interesting, is it?"

"Can I give you a lift?"

"No, I'll take a taxi."

Herbert smiled. "Sure. There's no reason you should trust me."

"You said it."

"See you soon," said Herbert, and he must have walked to where his car was parked because when Rose took a taxi she looked out of its back window and saw a dark blue BMW following them. As they drove up to the hotel, it paused, turned and drove away.

Rose didn't tell the old man any of this when she walked in. She gave him the two books and he looked through them, skimming pages and turning them as though he was looking for something.

"You've written novels and stories, haven't you?" Rose asked.

The old man didn't look up.

"Yes," he said, indifferent.

"So where are they? The books."

"I don't keep copies, one had to be careful. But we'll get them in the States if they are still in print." The old man looked up.

"There's a fortune there, you know. I didn't leave a literary executor." He could see she didn't understand. "I mean when the books sell, the writer gets some money and I didn't leave it to anyone, so they're holding it. But I tell you something, if they find a will with my signature and my old American attorney says that's authentic, then the money's coming to you. To my heir."

"But that's not where you get all this money you're throwing around."

"No. I'm not throwing it around, I'm trying to save our lives, girl."

She got the old man dressed and packed and they checked out of the hotel, called a cab and set off for Stratford. The amount of fuss he made handing out tips to the staff and having his bag brought in the same lift as the one he was descending in, calling for a taxi and asking silly questions, he must have drawn the attention of every bellboy and attendant in that hotel. The wrong way of trying to travel incognito, Rose thought.

Behind their taxi, all the way to Stratford there were two cars. One of them was the dark blue BMW and the other a small red British car.

From The Notebooks Of Simon Forman

A third and fourth plague struck London in the last years of the millennium and while doctors and others who profess themselves masters of disease and cure ran away, I battled with it. Many a time I suspected that being close-quartered to people who had caught the plague I had symptoms of it.

I have to report here that the plague caught the Marshalsea prison and many of the prisoners died. The Master Warden called me in for my assistance as he and his wife and daughter were also laid low by the pestilence. My curing of the warden was taken note of by the Lord Mayor and my book *Discourse On The Plague* has been widely read.

In the spring of 1603 I moved house from Southwark to that same Deptford where I bought a property.

I intend to keep a book of all the plays that I see from this day on, having the leisure to do so. I have been these years to see the Lord Chamberlain's Men act and also the Lord Admiral's Men. This company has now sold all its property, its plays and possessions, and closed down.

Part of my reason for venturing to Southwark to see plays was to find Master Lazarus or indeed Master Marlowe again. But I did not see them. I gained no intelligence of either for a long time. He sank like a pebble in an ocean and it seemed the waters closed above him.

In the years when the plague visited us three times, I saw and heard of the great rise of this Master Sebastian who was to be seen much in Southwark and Bankside in the company of Master Shakespeare, of my Lords Essex and Southampton.

In February of that fateful year there was much disturbance in Southwark. My Lord Monteagle had pressed the Chamberlain's Men to bring again to the stage the old play *Richard II* at The Globe. The play commenced in the afternoon and it was known that Essex's men had pressed for this play as example to the London mob. Here was a story in which a weak king who courted favorites sent a great and good man into exile and in which the exile came back and drove the weak monarch from the throne. Would Essex not have wanted the men of England to see that he could drive the Queen's favorites out of power and even depose the Queen?

Sebastian played the role of Richard's young Queen. Master Shakespeare absented himself from playing though Master Burbage, the younger, played Bolingbroke. I witnessed this performance at which there was a great deal of passion. Neither my Lord Essex nor my Lord Wriothesley, Earl of Southampton, attended.

That evening rumor had it that Essex had been summoned by the Council and warned of treason. Again word spread in the city that Essex had been defiant in the very face of the Council, calling them the miscreants. The next day at Essex House the Queen herself sent Lord Essex word through several nobles, the Lord Keeper, the Chief Justice, the Earl of Worcester and Sir William Knollys to plead with Essex and ask him to disband the host of followers and young men that waited on him, with arms and horses at the ready as though they would do rash deeds. Instead of giving way to their pleas, Essex, bold now with the feeling that the Queen was really worried about his rebellion, held all four of the messengers prisoner. Then he rode out with a few hundred of his men to Ludgate Hill and into the city. They brandished their swords and claimed that the Queen's courtiers, parasites and caterpillars, had laid a plot to kill Essex. They were out now not to attack but to defend their master against this plot.

Ludgate Hill was closed off by the Queen's force and though they raised their hand in treason against the throne, Essex was beaten off.

Several of the Chamberlains men were questioned by the Knight Marshall's Men and it is thought Sebastian and Master Shakespeare went into hiding. At any rate I saw them no more.

Essex, on being brought before the court, said he cared not. "I owe God a death," and it seemed many young men of the city cared more for his life than he did. The line was well noted. Some even noted that when the Chamberlain's Men had played *Henry VI,* the tailor in it speaks the same line.

The master of the Chamberlain's company was summoned. Master Shakespeare was called for but had, it was believed, retired to Stratford on Avon. The rebellion was not to be laid at his door. He had amused the Queen with several loyal plays and devices, including *A Midsummer Night's Dream* and *Much Ado About Nothing,* which were great favorites in court. And the Queen and the members of the Council had not forgotten *Two Gentlemen Of Verona* and *Love's Labours Lost* and *Love's Labours Regained,* which were played by children in the Queen's House each year.

Soon after the rebellion was put down, I was sent for by the warden of the Marshalsea. I thought perhaps he had more wretches for me to cut up. Not so. Among the wretches who had been brought to him for begging, men and women with no home and no parish to which they could be returned, was a black man who would say no word and, Master Warden said, had something about him of the air of Lazarus, though he was much transformed. This news was something of a shock. I went in haste to the Marshalsea. Sure enough it was Lazarus sitting under a cowl.

The warden said he had tried conversation with him and had offered him his freedom if he desired it. He had sat there this day and night without food. I looked at him. His face was deeply marked with scars which had healed in patterns and his hair, even though the man was not late into his thirty and some years, was gray.

And yet it was our Lazarus. Wrapped in the Marshalsea's cloth and almost naked but for this, he sat in a cell. He made no move when I approached him bearing a lantern in that dark. I asked Master Warden to withdraw.

I tried to speak to him but Lazarus made no motion nor gave any sign that he knew me. He looked up but there was no recognition in his eyes.

"Lazarus, you disappeared. Will you come home with me now?"

He made no reply.

"I made a lot of enquiry. I asked down by the dock if a man such as yourself had been seen sailing for France. What happened to you?"

Again he would make no reply.

"Many a time have I thought of you and I thought perhaps I had given you some offense and that caused you to run away. I even cast figures to enquire of the stars and discovered only that you had crossed the water and had found yourself in crowds and chains. I have been troubled to think you were imprisoned and now the warden tells me you were forced to beg. What need was there to beg? Your treasure is still in my house and you may return home when you wish."

He said nothing but he wept. Silently, with the tears coming down his cheeks.

"I beg of you come with me, sir. You are welcome. And I do not mean to ask you your adventures. I am ashamed to see you so degraded and would know the cause, but you may stay silent if it is your wish."

Lazarus fell upon my neck and I put the lamp down and held him.

He would come with me, he made assent, and again he spoke not.

The warden canceled the warrant of Lazarus's imprisonment when I said he would go with me under my protection.

I hired an extra horse and we rode out to Deptford to a house Lazarus had not been in before. I gave him clothes and hot water to wash. When he came to the table to eat, he took the meat and began to crush it in his palm and dip it in his cup of drink before he would swallow it. I asked him what he was doing. It was then he opened his mouth wide and stuck his tongue out. I could see the cause of his saying nothing. Anchored to his strong red tongue was the thick link of an iron chain. At first I thought it was some illusion, a trick, but on looking closely I saw that it pierced his tongue completely and was fast around it. By pulling in his tongue he could accommodate the link in his mouth, for it was larger than a crown and as thick as the nose ring of a bull. He showed me how he held it between his teeth and spoke nothing. The flesh of the tongue had grown around this link. Lazarus indicated with his hand that there had been more links in this chain. They had chained his tongue.

Who?

Lazarus slept that whole day and the next day he began to write the story for me.

The Adventures Of The Slave Lazarus Who Returned From Many Trials

AS TOLD TO MASTER FORMAN OF SOUTHWARK,
DOCTOR OF PHYSIC AND ASTROLOGY

I did not leave of my own free will. As you know I was lodging here when Master Marlowe sent me the plays to which I added, before giving them to Master Shakespeare. The appearance of the young Sebastian from France had disturbed me and raised some jealousy in me. I knew he was no player of any school, but had been a sailor, just by the way he stood and by his appearance and his rough manner of speech.

It was for the first time I felt the hot iron of jealousy pierce my heart. I felt nothing against this boy. Only anguish for myself and a mad desire to know! To know what they spoke to each other, how they touched, met, kissed. It was as deep as Hell this hunger to know more, everything. And I had no certain knowledge that they even knew each other. Yet, and yet Christopher who had sworn so many oaths to me, who had promised to return now or send for me — God, I knew that this boy had his favor.

My only proof — and how I clung to it — while wishing it wasn't true, was the pattern on the handkerchief that the boy pulled to wipe his brow at rehearsal. Did I fancy it or was he flaunting this kerchief? Was it not the one I gave Christopher after we had sold *The Rape Of Lucrece* to Master Field? I would know that handkerchief and pick it out if you strewed handkerchiefs like stars before me.

I burnt in this fury for a night and a day. Then I wrote my fears down. It was a letter to Christopher begging him to say it wasn't true. I left Master Forman's home at night and walked down to the wharf, to the taverns, looking for the man who brought me the plays and Christopher's note. If he was returning to France and found himself in Marseilles or Paris, could he convey this letter? I couldn't find that man.

I waited three days by the dock for any ship that might be bound for France or Spain. I must have been observed in every tavern in London from Southwark to Woolwich. It was after perhaps a week, one night on the quay by London Bridge, that four men approached me. I was standing by the embankment and saw them come. Two from each side of me. From the way they approached, something in their very footsteps, I knew they meant me harm. They passed close to me and one of them threw over me a net, such as they use for dredging. The others jumped on me with ropes and struck me with cudgels till I was nearly senseless. I cried out but they beat me till I was unconscious. I found myself tossed and churned in the hold of a ship. On the eighth day the ship docked in a Dutch port and two other men fetched me, bound and with a hood over my head.

What shall I tell you, Master Forman, they used me cruelly. I was chained and taken for a savage to the slave market. When a Dutchman looked at me for purchase they wished to look in my mouth and count my teeth. They took the bandage from my mouth and as soon as they had done that I was able to talk and shouted that I was no savage but a Christian and a free man who had been set upon by brigands. The man who would have paid money for me and taken me to the Indies again, heard me and asked my captors to set me free.

Of course they did not set me free. They whipped me and took me back into the hold and I fought them and shouted for help. They put stones in my mouth and bound my mouth up. Every time they tried to feed me, I would shout and they fed me less and less. But they knew that if they gave me no water I would die and their effort and trade would be lost, so they unbound my mouth and had to endure my shouting. Till on which day I know not, for the days and nights became just one to me, they brought a surgeon and holding me down they cut this hole in my tongue and a smith fixed the chain to its middle.

Not content with this barbarity, the surgeon made gashes in my cheeks and forehead so they could pass me off for a savage. It took an eternity for the pain in my mouth to abate. I prayed for death. I tried to dash my brains out but they bound me by the neck down to the floor of the hold. Throughout my wrists and ankles were bound together.

As I lay there, I saw other black men and women on their passage through that hell hole. From where they came and where they went I could not ask.

My day came when these Devil's disciples sold me to a performing show in which there were many monsters and many wild animals. I was kept in a cage. I had been, as I told you, in a lewd entertainment before, but Master Meade had never used me in this way. I was now put on the stage as a bear, as a lion, as a devil, as a madman. I have been a slave and sweated as a boy on the plantation of Hispaniola. But never has man been so degraded. I was kept in a cage.

Master Forman, I first raged with my chained mouth from which I could roar and make indistinct speech (at which they laughed) till I had no voice and then I went for weeks into a stupor. I tell you, human beings make of the space they are given a tolerable hell. I lived for two years or more in that cage and like an animal, I learnt what was least painful. When to stand, when to roar, when to rattle my chains. Never tell me that the spirit cannot be defeated. It may be alive but it can be curbed so easily. Our bodies are so frail. The rage in us rattles some bars, but cannot break out of the prison.

The vile men who owned this circus put animal skins upon me and feathers and hung my waist and shoulders with human bones and skulls to make the sight of me dreadful. And for the audience I danced. And my tongue was always out, chained, without language, like a bear being led.

Our cages were drawn by horse from town to town and we would come upon a common and wait there ten or twenty days and then the misery of creatures would move on again. I do not know all the places we went. A million faces passed that cage and gazed.

We encamped one day in France outside Paris. I never knew where we were. I had taught myself to be content that the sun rose every day and night came hours after I had longed for it.

And I saw them, Master Forman. Christopher was always addicted to such vile shows. Any form of human degradation he loves. He had grown a long beard and wore a wool cap over shortened hair in the style of a sailor and with him was Sebastian. He had paid his penny and was gazing. They walked as lovers do before the cage, hand in hand, an afternoon's amusement. Next to me the bears were being made to dance on their chains and somewhere in this fair they fed a cockerel to a young tiger and people watched the tiger fight the feathers and swallow them whole.

I can swear to you, Master Forman, that Christos looked into my eyes and he saw me there. He recognized me, but no shadow crossed his face. No surprise, no question, he stared. He was staring, his slim jaw set, at Fate itself.

I could not call out to him and he would say nothing to me. The moment was like an hour, but it must have been the merest glance. And maybe he did not see me. Maybe we only see what we expect to see and this circus creature, scarred, his tongue heavy with iron and neck and body hung with skulls and wearing bull's horns was far, far removed from anything he had loved. It was but a moment and then they were gone. From that day on I played for the crowd. I did tricks like an animal. What I ate I had to tear into pieces with my hands and swallow whole, for around the link I could not chew and my teeth began to ache. I was thrown raw meat to tear and thus to please the mob. I begged for pennies to please my masters. I became the friendly monster they had paid for. This place was my home now. For me, Master Forman, an ex-slave, I carry my home on my back and some times through life I find a house for this home. You have invited me in here and you did before with Christos.

It was religion that set me free. One night in a town called Magdeburg, a mob of Protestants came with burning torches on poles and with knives and staves to declare that our circus was an abomination and that we had put to sacrilegious use God's work of creation. It was blasphemy, as we were with animals and humans making mock of Noah's great boat, God's first circus. They smashed all the cages with hammers and some of the animals were burnt alive. The owners of the circus were caught and taken to face trial. I was set free.

One of the torch-bearers hammered the links of the chain off, all except this one which is embedded in my tongue. By many ways I made my way back to London, working and begging and eating only where I could. There is no peace for the poor. After months on the streets of London they culled me as a beggar and here you have found me. For which, God give you grace and I, your humble servant, give you thanks which I cannot speak.

From The Diary Of Simon Forman

It was in the bitter cold month of February, 1603 that Lazarus came back to me.

My first task was to procure a hard file and to make a hot poultice of herbs and cloves to numb the pain of Lazarus's tongue. The flesh around the link, which was now brown with rust and would have killed him, was slightly blue as are veins under the skin. I told him I would need assistance to hold him down and the next day brought with me two astrologers of my acquaintance, one of whom was also a man of curves.

We held Lazarus and after several hours of filing we broke the link and pulled it from the hole in his tongue. The blood gushed and immediately we held the tongue with tongs. The poor poor man cried out for God and mercy and we applied hot flax and balm to the bloody wound.

He blessed us and after twelve hours of rolling in agony, he was exhausted and sweating and he slept.

For six months, till Michaelmas, this wound did not heal and Lazarus would slowly practice his speech.

He would not walk forth in the town till it was restored and then he bade me go with him. The spirit was not dead in him and he wanted to see the theater.

The play we went to see was advertised as *"The Famous Historie Of Troilus and Cresseid.* Excellently expressing the beginning of their loves with the conceived wooing of Pandarus Prince of Licia, written by William Shakespeare."

This play is full of general musing on time and what it does to love and spirit and reputation. The speech is not that which any other poet could have written. For me, as for Lazarus, there could be no doubt. There was Master Shakespeare himself and Burbage the younger and in the part of Cressida was the young man Sebastian. It was an ill-chosen play for Lazarus's first step into a new life. It told the story of love sworn and forsworn. Cressida, taken hostage by the Greeks, swears she will remain true to her love for Troilus and time eats away at this love till she loves Troilus not and loves Diomed, her captor. Time swallows love and faith as it had perhaps done the love and faith of one whom Lazarus should forget but of whom every line of the play was a reminder.

The groundlings did not love the play. I said to Lazarus we must away before nightfall, but he would stay.

"And the matter of the play?"

"I must acquaint myself with Master Shakespeare again. It was excellently done."

"Now don't be a fool, Lazarus, you must come home."

"Since I left here, it seems Master Shakespeare has learnt some philosophy. Or perhaps he buys his wit as one would one's loaf of bread, fully baked."

"And you find the baker?"

"Whatever I hear from Master Will, I shall go to his house in Clerkenwell and thence return home."

"Your home it is," I said.

Lazarus returned in a day. He looked sullen and full of thought and for a few days he shunned company. He was always civil to me but now he kept his own thoughts.

"Did you see Master Shakespeare in Clerkenwell as you intended?"

"My brother and friend, I cannot lie to you. I did not intend to see Will. I followed that Jack, the boy Sebastian to where he would go that evening. He went drinking at the King's Head and there was brought a horse by a serving man. He was about to ride out when I, having no horse, borrowed one from the stables in the yard of the inn. In short I stole one. I rode behind him and my inclination was correct. He rode south on the Kent road to Chiselhurst and Scadbury, to that very same estate of Sir Thomas Walsingham where you found me. He reached the house and I dismounted and, tying my horse walked the rest of the way in the dark. I went silently like a thief and I was rewarded as a thief should be with punishment. I heard *his* voice and the young Sebastian's which was ringing in my ear over and over, saying the lines of the wretched Cressida. The voices mingled in laughter. Christo's. He is here in England. You knew this?"

"I knew nothing of it."

"He is at the house of Lord Walsingham, who of course questioned Ingram Frizer, his servant, and in time was told that Kit is indeed alive."

"Perhaps you were mistaken, it may not have been his voice."

Lazarus shook his head. His eyes blinked hard. Was he forcing back tears or making a resolve in anger? I could not tell.

"I should not have followed the boy. I knew what I would find, but like the whipped dog that returns to lick the hand that carries the whip, I went. I wanted an end to it."

"To what?"

"To having no home. Twice I have found a new tongue. Once when Mr. Walsh brought me from Hispaniola and once when you set my tongue free from the chain. I have followed my tongue. This England has become the place where I can speak, but it is not my home. I thought till this last night that home would be where Master Marlowe was. Never mind that he did not see me in the monster of the circus. Never mind that he loves another. My spirit has nothing to return to."

"It can return to work, to writing plays, to being my apprentice in the arts of physic and prediction . . ."

"Plays? Must I write plays for Master Shakespeare? Would the Chamberlain's Men accept plays to present at court from a man who has been condemned for piracy and lives only under a trap-door of falsehoods, beneath the stage? Brother Simon, I swear, at least for this hour and this day, there is a burning in me, which will not die till he is not near any longer. I am a moth to a flame. I can put out the flame."

For a moment I thought he was full of fury, but his voice was calm and strong.

"The truth, of course, is the flame in me is dead. I shall play no hero. Instead I shall practice arts with you and I shall go back to the Chamberlain's Men and earn a shilling or two holding a spear in the crowd or a cushion with a jewel upon it, fair part for a black slave."

Master Shakespeare is now attended upon by men of all sorts. He is constantly in the company of the servants of Southampton who bring him to my house in the belief that he is seeking figures of fortune from me. He was with all his heart happy to see Lazarus and know that he was alive. Often in the years when Lazarus was in captivity, he would ask after him. Now he works with him upon a new play.

In the city other poets and writers of plays wonder at Master Shakespeare's great fecundity. He brings forth plays out of season, like a bush that would flower all year and feels every weather to be spring.

I am kept busy by the pestilence which breaks out again. I am busy letting blood, examining the urine and looking at the sores and poxes that afflict those with the pestilence. The Lord Mayor has issued an order that they be left alone. He need not have done it. Those with the plague stink. They stink of dried fish and of rotting wheat and of the sweet sickly smell of weeds that have died and festered.

Lazarus makes no mention of Master Marlowe. He has found employment again with the Chamberlain's Men who welcomed him as a lost and prodigal brother.

With Will Shakespeare, Lazarus says, he is writing a tragedy that will shake all London. It is complete. Master Shakespeare would take it to Burbage even that day, but Lazarus is cautious. There are companies who send out actors as spies to find out what other companies are doing. The actors must be given individual parts and no one man should see the whole. So over three days and several flasks of wine Master Shakespeare, Lazarus and I, copy each man's parts and lines on to separate sheets. Armed with these, Master Shakespeare gets to the Globe and the next day Lazarus is summoned.

He is to play in this latest tragedy of a Moor of Venice, general of the Venetian army. He reads the part to Master Burbage and tells that he will play the part but he must know how the tragedy begins and progresses. He asks that he may see the other parts, but Master Burbage will retain them secret.

By the day the rehearsals are done and the play is to be shown, Lazarus has grown his hair in a white bush and now he oils it and combs it down magnificently like a lion's mane at the back. Yet it stands proud and curly in front like a crown of thorns. He smiles much nowadays and has taken to wearing a mixture of oil and lead to darken the lower parts of his eyelids. His tongue is active and booms in the hollow of his mouth. No one would suspect that there is still a scar and a dent in that tongue where it had been pierced by iron.

The first day the play comes on it amazes all London. Word goes out that Lazarus has performed magnificently.

"I have not read this masterpiece, but I shall now attend the play."

Lazarus bows. "In my heart it is dedicated to you. Tell me, my friend, have you ever in all your work with the afflicted ever caught the fever yourself?"

I tell him that I have felt it coming on. "But then I administered to myself and bled myself and brought my biles in balance again and I was cured."

"So physicians may heal themselves?"

"Sometimes, Lazarus, they do it by healing others. I put myself to work and the fever leaves me."

"I have done the same," says Lazarus, "but I am not sure of the cure."

Othello, for such is the name of the play, is the greatest test of the sin of jealousy ever offered in poem or play or indeed in sermons or in the holy book itself. Word travels and it certainly travels to Chiselhurst. It is a triumph of a play.

Since I helped to transpose it, certain characters are altered and certain lines have changed in the staging. Perhaps Master Shakespeare, like the tailor with a garment already made, has pulled a stitch here and a hem there. I go on three occasions.

And who is this who with a hat and feather and a mask to hide his eyes, and with a sharp fair chin sits in the box by the side of the stage with my Lord Walsingham and his lady? And why today is there a coming and going of several actors from the stage before the play begins to observe the crowd, as it were, and determine when to start? And why have trumpeters been instructed today to blow a march before the play begins?

For all that, the play starts late and proceeds as I have seen it. There is William Kemp taking a part and Henry Condell and in the part of the young Cassio there is a handsome young actor barely a boy fresh out of a choir. Then there is in fine lace and with a voice that would tease, the other boy of the company, Sebastian, who plays Desdemona.

Lazarus's eyes pierce me. There is a fire burning there, the fever of the brain. He speaks his lines, not like an actor but like a man giving testimony before the lord on judgement day, with fear for the judgement.

I am to blame. Simon Forman, who knows the character from the shape of the knuckles, who reads the fates from signs and marks on the palm, who casts figures; the same Simon, I am he. And the man Lazarus, Walsh's Henry, hopeless boy, brought by pirates to this country, rescued from death, resurrected, he lives in my house and I restore him to his being and I read nothing of him. Nothing.

On stage there comes the scene of night and Othello enters the bedchamber where Sebastian frets. He calls to the chaste stars. There are only torches on stage. The evening sky above the theater is by now darkening. In a simple white robe Othello gently raves. He is a man with his mind made up. He has made peace with his God, his conscious and his face and words only serve to still his beating heart and the tumult of his blood. He is to kill her. He picks up the pillows and smothers Desdemona.

Now he draws his Spanish sword and is saying that all he did was done in honor and not in hate.

The others are on the stage and Othello talks to me, directly to me. He is looking at me.

"When you do these unlucky deeds relate
Speak of me as I am. . . ."

Now he grabs himself by the throat and with the other hand plunges the dagger into the back of his neck. The other players pause for him and he stumbles forward. A low moan, long and melancholy, of despair more than pain, escapes him and he falls, hinged by his feet like a great tree that is felled.

The crowd gasps. This has been counterfeit but as near to the real as men want to see.

The scene finishes and the play. The figure in the box with the mask stays unmoving as the audience applaud and shout and caps are thrown in the air. The players come to the edge of the stage to take applause but Othello lies still.

In that moment I know. I push myself to the front of the crowd. One of the players is kneeling by him. This man presumes that Lazarus is overcome by the great labor, but I climb on to the stage. The blood seeps out from the back of his neck and then as the players gather the alarm goes up.

"He has done himself a mischief. A surgeon, quick."

Sebastian flees from the stage in horror. The crowd do not know what has happened. I turn the body over. There is a gash where the backbone joins the skull and the blood flows from it.

He has no pulse, no breath.

"The slave has killed himself. Do not touch the body till the Marshall's men have satisfied themselves."

"He lodged with me. I am his next of kin," I say, but the Company's men push everyone from the stage. The Marshall's men arrive and there is talk of an inquest the following day. The body must rest there in the theater under their guard.

So ended the story of Lazarus save to say that the body disappeared the next day. The guard was asleep and it was thought that the slave's black body had been stolen for withcraft.

I heard no more of Master Marlowe either, but saw his boy Sebastian on stage when the King's charter came to the

Chamberlain's Men and the company became the King's Men. Soon after they did the play called *Measure For Measure*. Whether it was Master Marlowe I cannot say, but three years later a play came into my possession, brought to me by the hand of a young and poor-looking lass who would answer no questions. It was entitled *Antony And Cleopatra*. I knew not what to do with this play but read it and took it to the King's Men. Master Shakespeare would not see me, so I left it in the hands of others to convey to him and wrote him a letter, to say I had chanced upon this play in the personal belongings of an old friend. Whomsoever sent me the play did not want Master Shakespeare to make any enquiry. That is all I could conclude from it having been sent to me.

Two further plays came to me entitled *Macbeth* and *Cymbeline* and I sent them again as I had to Master S, taking care to keep a copy for myself. I gathered these later in a *Book Of Plays*.

In 1609 I was interested to see that I had been sent a copy of the published *Sonnets of William Shakespeare*. Poor old William Shakespeare, who never in his life rhymed rat with cat. Here he is confessing his loves and as I knew him his only marriage was to a lady of sharp tongue in Stratford and his only love was the bottle.

I take note of the Sonnets which are printed by Thomas Thorpe, a rogue well-known to me for giving writers no royalties for their work. They are dedicated to Mr. W.H. My particular favorites are the numbers XX, CXXVII and CXLVII as all these hold the secret I have here laid bare.

ROSE SAT by the window of the bedroom in the luxury suite of the hotel in Stratford. She could see, as in a picture book, the river, the bridge, the swans. The old man sat up in bed.

"And I suppose that's the end," he said. "Shall we leave it there?"

He hadn't read this last chapter from any manuscript. He had dictated it straight, all in one sitting. He asked Rose to make some tea and then go out and get some champagne. Again they would celebrate.

"If we order the best champagne they have, it will again draw attention to ourselves. You must go out and get it. It'll teach you to buy wine, anyway. Go and ask for the best shop in the market and get some Dom Perignon, twenty or more years old. They must have something like that. A very good indication of whether a wine is any good is the price. People in this backward place are finally learning about wines."

"Is that the end of the story?"

"I suppose it is."

"What about the stuff I dug up in London, the Marlowe sonnet on the church stone?"

"Well, it's clear isn't it?"

"There were two endings."

"Sure, child. The one you found on the church stone is the more truthful. It says the eclipse blots out the sun, the black shades out the bright, so the low or poor or someone who was a slave can bring discredit on the work of the mightier one. What do you think it means?"

"It's obvious. It means the plays that Marlowe wrote may not be thought as good as those written by Lazarus."

"Who do you think wrote it?"

"Marlowe? Simon Forman? Whose grave is it supposed to be?"

"I am sure it is that of Lazarus."

"Do you think he killed himself on stage?"

"Forman simply says a young lass came and gave him some folios of plays. Who was she? Did Lazarus arise from the dead once again and take some poor girl for a wife?"

"What about the window in my school chapel? The stained-glass picture?"

"That should be obvious. Marlowe must have done penance for having caused the death of Lazarus, for he blamed himself. He must have passed the story on and the Marlowe players who founded your school must have known it."

"But Marlowe himself was an atheist."

"Dear child, people are not this or that. They do unexpected things. Even in his own times, whenever *Doctor Faustus* was performed, strange things happened. Was it the dead slave's curse?"

"What you never said was whether Lazarus really killed himself or whether he used his tricks again, of breathing and bleeding and playing dead."

"I made it as clear as I could, or as clear as I want to."

"That's for the public," Rose said, "I am going to defend the story, remember?"

The old man grinned.

"Oh, you are? So you accept then? You'll be adopted and take my name and be my daughter?"

"I didn't say that. I just said I have to know what happened to Lazarus."

"You know the first Lazarus," Mr. B said. "Well, a friend of mine wrote a poet about the raising of Lazarus by Jesus. The point of the poem was that Jesus brought him round once, but never asked why he'd died, and never took the suicide tablets from his coat!"

"You mean one day Lazarus was bound to die, so it might as well have been on that stage playing Othello?"

"Maybe."

"And Marlowe?"

"We think we know where he is buried. He wrote several plays before that. One curious thing. When Simon Forman was an old man, a woman approached him on the streets of London saying she had brought with her a parcel from Paris in which he would be interested. He asked what it was. She produced from a box the decaying head of a man whom he recognized as Kit Marlowe, bald now, and with holes for eyes. Forman asked her 'Who are you?' and she replied, 'I am one whose death you arranged. I have lived in France all these years because my life was in danger here in London. I was sought after by vile men and fled to save myself. My name is Lilly Camby.' "

As Rose stepped out of the hotel she saw Herbert sitting on the river bank reading a book, looking out for her.

"I expected you to be here," she said, and then, "I don't know why I talk to you. You're some kind of villain and you probably want to kill Mr. . . . . him."

"Do I look like that?"

Rose didn't reply.

"Can I walk with you?"

"If you like. Don't you want to sit and watch to see he doesn't run away?"

Herbert pointed to a car parked on the opposite side of the river and to another parked at the gate. There were men sitting in both.

"Is that what you people do for a living? Follow people around?"

"No, actually. I'm a model. Well, they photograph me for things. And I'm a student."

"You a student?" Rose was amazed.

"Yeah, I'm at the Poly."

"Doing what?"

"English literature, as it happens. Special subject? Not Caribbean literature, Elizabethan playwrights."

Rose wanted to ask why, but didn't.

"Funny, I want to go into a bookshop. Any one in Stratford I suppose."

"He wants more books?"

"Me. I thought I'd get some light reading while I wait for you to swoop."

"Swoop what? I've only been winding you up. I'm not looking for the old man at all. I'm actually a rich African prince and I've been following you because . . . you know."

"Well. Too bad. Because I think I know the solution to your riddle."

Rose could tell he was going to carry the joke on, but this stopped him dead in his tracks.

"What do you mean? Don't be silly."

"I'm not being silly. What do I get for the solution?"

Herbert thought for a couple of seconds.

"How about a quarter? There must be a million pounds there."

"And how do I know you'll be straight with me?"

"You can't know, you'll just have to take that chance."

"And what about the old man?"

"He doesn't need to sit on all that bread."

"What'll you do with him?"

"We could see him all right. He doesn't need much."

"He wants to go to America and buy a house and maybe a boat. What's it to you?"

"That's bad for the old boy because we're not going to go that far. We'll give him a pension and let him live like other old writers."

"I can keep the secret to myself."

"You could but my mates wouldn't like it. They're turning nasty, and how far can you go?"

"I thought that's almost exactly what you'd say."

"Is it a number? It could be a number or it could be a further clue. If it's a number we need two letters for the bank and then a number, maybe eight digits. Then we've cracked it."

Rose bought the champagne and Herbert watched her. He was slightly amused, she could see.

They went into a bookshop and Rose found a copy of

Shakespeare's *Sonnets.* Herbert said, "Let me pay for this so you can remember me in Stratford."

They went to a coffee shop which was crammed with German tourists. Rose decided.

"Do you have a copy of the poem?"

Of course he had. He spread it out on the table between them.

"I don't need a copy, I know it backwards and sideways."

"Okay, it's one word from each of the lines, reading backwards," Rose said.

"I worked that one out. Because the first two words are Account No. Then we've traced all sorts of combinations of the words."

"Let me show you. It goes something like this."

Rose took out her pen and underlined words.

"If you know what you're doing, you can find things."

She underlined "lover" and "Dark" from the first and second lines.

"Now take the third and fourth lines. 'I leave this verse to grace and empty grave/A reference point to say "A life is done." ' Which words would you underline from those? They stand out."

" 'Verse' and 'Reference' I suppose, because we're looking for references to sonnets," said Herbert.

"You are getting on fine. The meaning of the next is clear — look for a name and a date. But how? Okay, the following lines: 'To piece together a picture which can tell/You more about him than the poems or prose/He left behind. Of all the souls in hell/(The numbers grow) he rises from the deep . . .' Go on then, which words?"

"I think I go for 'piece together,' 'poems,' 'numbers,' 'all.' "

"Not bad," said Rose. "Could do better. But what do you think it means?"

"It means take the numbers of the sonnets that have a dark lover in them and piece them together."

"But there are lots of dark lover sonnets. Which ones?"

Herbert took up the book of sonnets and leafed through it.

"Christ. I don't know. Why don't you just borrow a gun from me and ask the old man?"

"You carry a gun?"

"It was only a joke."

They finished their coffee and went into the street.

"I don't need the gun anyway. I think I know the answer. The old man gave it to me," Rose said.

"How?"

"You were spot on. Through the story. Forman gets the sonnets and he says his favorite ones. Last sentence of the diary says: 'These hold the secret I have here laid bare.' "

Herbert grabbed Rose by the wrist.

"Sit down. Right here."

He forced her down on to the pavement. The tourists stared.

"Lovers in Stratford, let them stare. Lovers reading sonnets. Come on, the numbers."

He put his arm around her. Rose knew she didn't mind. She opened the book to Sonnet Number 20. They read it together.

" 'A man in hue all hues in his controlling.' " Herbert read the line. "Wow, we're getting there."

"Next, Number 127," said Rose.

Herbert read the first line: " 'In the old age black was

not counted fair . . .' Great, that one's in! And then?"

"And then we try Number 147 — the final favorite of Simon Forman."

They turned the pages, their fingers overlapping and interfering. They read through it silently and the last two lines together aloud: " 'For I have sworn thee fair, and thought thee bright,/Who are as black as hell, as dark as night.' "

"I think that's it. The jackpot!" Herbert said.

A Japanese couple looked at them as they sat on the pavement, the cars passing by.

"We feel like a million bucks," said Herbert to them and they smiled politely.

"You forgot the two letters," said Rose.

"They couldn't be anything else could they? W and H. I'm not that stupid."

They got up from the pavement.

"What do you have to do now?" asked Rose.

"Take a trip to Zurich. His signature is not a problem, you can get that for us. But we've cracked it."

Rose didn't say anything.

"And I'm not going back on anything. The money's yours. Get the old man back to London. You just quit and come with me and and we'll write him a note and send a car and driver to bring him back. You come with me to Zurich."

"You're mad. I can't just ditch the old man."

"Think of what you can do for your mother. It wasn't the old man's bread anyway. He stole it. So he can't do anything about it."

Rose thought for a minute.

"Give him a quarter."

"Done."

"What about the rest of your gang?"

"Nothing about them. They can't read Shakespeare's sonnets or Marlowe's sonnets or nothing. They'll have to go to school."

"But won't they want the money?"

"Money? You think I told them about the money? They think I'm protecting the old man from some political conspiracy to kill him."

"But they'll find out we've got the money."

"Then we'll just have to disappear."

They walked along the banks of the Avon. Opposite the hotel Herbert pointed out a black swan.

"I'd be stealing from myself." Rose said.

"What do you mean?"

"The old man wants to adopt me. Pass all his money on to me legally."

"The old man is crazy," Herbert said. "Do you know how many people he's promised that to? He started with Angelina Trench. He met her when he was in America. He promised her the world and then he ended up stealing the island's wealth. You know what he told her to get out of that one? That his life was in danger and he couldn't marry her because it wouldn't be fair to make a widow of her. What a jerk!"

"And you?" Rose asked. "He promised it to you too, didn't he?"

"More than that, Rose. I told you, I grew up in London and didn't know nothing else. Like the rest of my black mob, I didn't get any exams, I just hung out and chilled out in them days. Clubs, the circuit. We didn't want to work at London Transport, so we had to make some bread, whichever way was quickest, you know. We used to climb in through the roofs of electronic shops and steal the gear. The burglar alarms were always on the walls, so we went in vertically. Got caught a few times and blamed the cops for planting us. You know the scene. But I got fed up of being poor and busted and without any ideas. It was ideas I was looking for and the guys I used to hang around with had run clean out of them. So I joined the revolution. Right on sister." Herbert did a black power salute.

"I got into it. That was when they sent me as a sort of army trainee, a 'cadre' they called it, to Santa Bella. I had three, four good years there, man. My dad comes from Santa Bella, so I'd always heard how fantastic it was, even though my dad never wanted to return to it — just talk about it while living happily in Loughborough Junction, Lambeth, London. I was full of it. I became part of the government guard, you know. Two months gun training, six months 'elite' training, all that. We went to Cuba for a week of cadre school and then I came out with government ministers as a bodyguard.

That's when I got to know the old man. I had a good time, but they messed it up, didn't they — the revolutionaries, they fought each other and started shooting each other. Then the Yanks came and wiped it all out. Then you know the rest. I might have got arrested, so I got to Trinidad and then back to London. Of course, by that time I knew I had to find the old man, find the money."

"You've done a lot," Rose said. She was genuinely impressed by the story.

"Not thirty-one for nothing. But now a new chapter begins, right? With you, Rosey, partners, you know?"

"I'm not sure, Herbie, let me talk to the old man."

"OK. I respect that," Herbert said. "But remember I got the numbers and I can get to Switzerland fast, so don't take your time."

Rose felt she knew this kind of young man. He was the kind of London lad who could have been her brother, or a neighbor. She felt a comfortable familiarity with him, as though she had known him for years.

There was no answer when Rose knocked at the door. Then she tried it, thinking the old man may have fallen asleep.

She called out and banged on the door. After a minute or so she decided that Mr. B may have stepped out for a bit of fresh air. After all, he hadn't left the inside of his own room for years and the sudden outing may have renewed his interest in not being cooped up. She returned to the elevators and down to the hotel lobby. She looked in the garden, where there was a bar and some tennis courts. There was hardly anyone there and certainly no sign of Mr. B. She headed for the roof garden.

As she went up in the elevator she had the funny, sinking feeling that the old man had run away. She went back down to the lobby and asked if the old man had checked out. They said he had, fifteen or twenty minutes before. He'd called for a taxi and had paid both their bills till the next day.

Had he left a note?

Nothing. The desk clerks looked at Rose curiously. She asked if she could look in his room.

It had been cleaned. There was nothing there, the clerk said.

Rose rushed out of the hotel. She'd get a taxi to the airport. She rushed back and grabbed her bag with the few clothes she'd brought. She knew where he'd go.

On the way to the airport she panicked. Why was she following this daft old man? She could easily just go home to London. She decided she ought at least to get to the airport and confront Mr. B. Why had he run away? Why had he not told her the truth about himself?

She was furious. She felt like giving him a slap and hurting him, shouting at him for behaving in the most childish and untrusting way.

At the airport Rose rushed to the information desk. Was there a direct flight to Switzerland that day? There were several. And the last one, when had it left? About five minutes before. The next one? No more flights today, miss, tomorrow, ten-thirty in the morning. She could fly to Frankfurt and change if she had to get to Zurich tonight.

The bastard, he had outsmarted her. Rose turned from the desk. Herbert was standing behind her.

"He's done a runner, hasn't he?"

"How did you get here?"

"I'm living in my car outside your hotel, I saw you running for a cab, so I followed you. He's gone, hasn't he?"

Rose nodded.

"What are you going to do?"

"Get back to London and my mother," Rose said.

"You can't pack it in now. The old devil can't be let off so lightly. Let's go to Zurich."

"For what?"

"How you mean for what? For the million or so pounds."

"He'll have got hold of it."

"We'll see about that."

"I'm amazed he even got himself dressed and on to a plane. How will he manage in Switzerland by himself?"

"Is that what bothers you? He's run a whole country, girl, he's a bit feeble, but . . . what's the matter?"

Rose was looking puzzled and sad.

"You look as though someone had died."

"Perhaps someone has."

"Come on. I've got plastic money, let's buy a holiday in Zurich."

Rose decided she had nothing to lose. She wanted some answers from the old man.

By the time they got into Zurich it was late evening.

"Maybe he's not here at all, maybe he went to New York or even back to London," Rose said. "How are we going to find him?"

"Just one clue," Herbert replied. "When he was education minister in the Santa Bella government, he came here once for a United Nations conference on culture. I came with the delegation as a bodyguard. We stayed at the swishest diplomatic hotel, to prove that socialists were as good as the rest of them, and the old man gave a speech on Shakespeare and the importance of the western intellectual tradition to the West Indies. I remember the speech. I was at the foot of the stage, dressed in khaki with a sten gun and dark glasses. We used to imitate the Cubans and guys in the government all thought they were Fidel Castro at least, if not Lenin. The old man enjoyed it. There were other Caribbean countries, Jamaica and Trinidad and Guyana and the Africans were there and they were all talking about the roots of their culture in Africa.

"Mr. J got up and said it was a load of humbug, slavery and its legacy were great historical tragedies, but for the past two hundred years or so, the Caribbean had been part of America and of European culture. I remember the words: 'Let's be honest, what do we have? We ex-slaves? We may have some sentimental attachment to Africa, but we have given the world a few things in the modern age. A few world class cricketers. (There was a great cheer from the Caribbeans and even the British and Australians and Indians and such.) Some international writers, like V. S. Naipaul, C.L.R. James, Wilson Harris, others. Nothing much more!'

"Oh God help us, man, there was an uproar. The black delegations began to scream. They got on their feet and booed him. Others stood and cheered, the whites, the Americans. I thought it was the closest we, me and the other pretend bodyguards, had come to actually defending our man. I thought he was going to get mobbed.

"Later that evening and all next day, the notes, flowers, abusive phone calls, threats, all sorts, came through his suite at the hotel.

"He called the delegation together. He was very arrogant: 'I don't know if you understood everything I had to say from the platform, comrades, but we have them on the run, boys!" He was overjoyed at the reaction."

"Okay, I know what you mean," Rose said. "I know him too. He'll be at that hotel."

"Makes sense. He's lived in isolation, running from us all these years. He'll want to relive his crowded hour."

They drove in a taxi to the hotel.

They booked separate rooms and then Herbert asked the clerk whether a Mr. Johnson was in a particular suite. There was no Mr. Johnson there. Herbert tried a few other names. The clerk politely looked through the register.

"Is there a Mr. Lazarus staying at the hotel?" Rose asked.

The clerk didn't have to check the computer. "Ah yes, Mr. Lazarus is here." The clerk smiled.

"Nice one," Herbert said to Rose.

"Can we have the room number, please?"

Again without looking, the clerk said, "Charter Suite One, seventh floor. Shall I ring him for you?"

"No, no, please don't."

The clerk looked at his watch.

"It's fine," he said. "Mr. Lazarus left instructions that no enquiry concerning him was to be answered till seven o'clock. It is now three minutes past nine."

They thanked the clerk and took the baggage to the elevators.

"Let me go in first," Rose said.

Herbert nodded. "I'll be in my room."

Rose went up to the seventh floor, leaving her bag with Herbert.

She found the suite and knocked. The old man's voice answered, almost cheerily, "Come in."

"Ah, Rosey, I was expecting you. Too late, man, the money transferred and the new number is here, right here." He tapped his forehead.

Rose walked into the huge suite. The old man was half lying, half sitting up in the huge king-size bed. It looked as though he had on three sweaters. He'd pulled the blankets right up to his chin and there was the mess of a box of tissues lying all round the bed and on it. Rose resisted her instinct to clean up the mess. She went and stood by the bed.

"I don't care about the money, Mr. B, but why did you run away?"

"Sit down, get yourself a drink. We've got some talking to do." The old man motioned towards the cabinet which concealed a fridge.

Rose got herself some lemon juice.

"All this running about has given me fever, man."

Rose sat at the edge of the bed. The old man's eyes were watering. He didn't look at all well.

"I bought myself some sweaters as soon as I came out of the bank."

"Why? Just tell me why?"

"I saw you, man, I saw you. I went up to the terrace garden for a little drink and a look around. Man, I had a good look around. Stratford looks quaint from up the terrace of the hotel. The theater which looks like some large garage and the willows washing in the river and the swans. I saw a couple of black swans, floating down the Avon. Then I spotted you, moving with the boy Shaka — that's what he called himself in those days, but his real name was Herbert. I thought to myself, so she's been in on the plot from the start and I've been a fool and let her infiltrate my house, my thoughts, my story, my secret."

"Wrong, Mr. B. Quite wrong."

"Well, right or wrong, it doesn't matter now, does it? The money is safe. You plotters won't get your hands on it."

"Yes, all right, keep your money. Believe it or not, I never met Herbert before you sent me to Dr. Trench's. Of course he had been waiting for you to show up there. He knew that she was the only doctor you'd trust. Nothing to do with me. I was just working for you and believing everything you told me. And you told me a lot of lies." As she spoke Rose realized that she was genuinely angry with the old man. She felt deceived and betrayed.

"You didn't tell me that you stole the money, did you? And then all that bullshit about adopting me."

"That wasn't a lie, my dear," the old man said, feebly. He looked stunned at Rose's reaction.

"Of course it was. You can't legally adopt me, you must

have known that. You can't because you don't legally exist! You, whoever you are, walked off a beach and have been certified dead. How can you adopt anyone? Ridiculous!"

For a moment the old man was quiet.

"You're right, in that sense, Rosey," he said after a while, "I didn't mean adopt in that way. I meant you could have this money, but more than that. I meant we should be soul companions, that you more than anyone understand the story I'm telling."

"Why does the story matter?"

"Because stories always matter. Because it's my story. I don't mean I invented it, I mean, it's my own story."

"I know that. Well, parts of it," Rose said.

"You don't think I'm crazy do you, Rosey?" the old man asked.

"It had occurred to me," Rose replied.

"I knew he and you would follow me here."

"And you booked the obvious hotel and registered in the obvious name?"

"Yes."

"So you wanted us to find you?"

Mr. B didn't reply. Instead he said, "This feller Herbert, you like him, don't you?"

"I don't know him at all, to tell the truth."

"I'll tell you what I'm thinking. I don't want to run around the world dodging these fellers. You never know what they might do. They might shoot me. Worse, they might think I've given you the cash and come after you. I've been thinking I might do a deal with them."

"That's up to you," said Rose. "I've got the answer I wanted. I think I'll have a good night's rest and I'll get to London in the morning and go to university and study drama and hope that Mom's okay. If you get back to London, send the Inspector or someone round to say how you are. I'm sure Mom will be interested."

Rose stood up and started to leave the room. She had a strong urge to be out of there, out of this game, away from Herbert and the old man and the deal with money and everything.

"You said *King Lear* was your favorite play," the old man said, his voice hoarse.

Rose turned.

"So?"

"The old man, his daughters . . . you know the play . . . a foolish old man."

"It's only a play," said Rose. "Good night, Mr. B."

Rose walked down the corridor and went to her own room. She called Herbert.

He was anxious.

"He is going to make a deal with you, so you better see him tomorrow morning," Rose said.

"How about you?"

"I want nothing to do with it. I'll be there, but I'm going back home tomorrow. Leave me out. I'm tired now. I want to sleep."

Her voice was firm and Herbert didn't argue. He said okay and wished her good night. If she knew him, he'd keep watch over the old man all night, to see he didn't get away again.

Rose didn't sleep. She sat on her bed thinking. A few hours passed. She may have dozed off because the next thing she heard was Herbert's voice and a knocking on her door.

"The old man. He's had a doctor and a nurse going in." Herbert had been watching the room.

Rose rushed to the seventh floor. The door to the old man's

suite was open and she and Herbert went in. There was one light on and a doctor, a nurse, and a hotel official who asked Rose what they wanted.

"I am his granddaughter," Rose said.

"Mr. Lazarus, your granddaughter's here," the doctor said to the old man, practically shouting in his ear.

The doctor turned to Rose. "We have to take him to the hospital. You can travel with us in the ambulance. He knew something was wrong and he called the desk."

Rose went with the ambulance. Mr. B was unconscious all the way. Rose prayed he'd regain consciousness. She had been vicious to him. She sat by the bedside at the hospital right through the next day. They put him on machines, strapped his wrists and plugged his chest to electronic machines and put oxygen masks on his face. He looked pale below the plastic.

The old man died that evening without opening his eyes. Rose went back to the hotel to pick up his things. Herbert said he'd help with whatever was needed.

There were his clothes. And there was, in the wardrobe, the manuscript that Rose had typed.

She opened it. On top, in a scrawl, was a letter to her. It said:

> Rosey, forgive my little test. You passed. I did
> change the account, but not the bank or the
> number, only the name and the signature. I've kept
> a bit for myself. I'm going back to the Caribbean
> and if I'm alive in a few years, visit me. Now dear
> child, you accused me wrongly. The money was not
> stolen, it was held in trust by me and now you. If
> you feel guilty, give the boys and Herbert some of

it, say a few hundred thousand. The rest is yours.
Enjoy it, look after your mother and thank her from
me and if I don't see you, have a good life.
Love,
Mr. B.

The handwriting was very difficult to read, it was scrawled
over four sheets of hotel paper.

Rose and Herbert stayed three more days in Zurich. On the
third day Rose visited the bank. The money was there, in her
name. The bank account had the number they had discovered. The bank manager had a copy of her signature on a
scrap of paper torn off the end of a note. It just said "Rose."
The old man must have torn it off a note she left him.

"That is your sample signature?" the manager asked.

"Yes, it is."

Rose and Herbert decided that Mr. B should be buried in
Santa Bella. Herbert made the arrangements. He was going
to accompany the remains; maybe stay there.

Back in London, with Mom at home now, packing her new
clothes to go away to Bristol to study drama, Rose reread the
manuscript. She made some changes. She had all the books
from his library and she read all the novels which had anything to do with the Caribbean. Six of them had a style she
recognized. The novels were written under a different name
— not Johnson, not Bernier, not any of the names on the
passports. Perhaps it was the old man's real name. Rose sent

the manuscript to the publisher and wrote a note to say that the old man was dead and had left this manuscript, would they publish it? They returned the manuscript with a letter:

Dear Ms. Hassan,

The author whose manuscript you claim to represent has been dead for fifteen years. The original editor of his books has read your manuscript and thinks you have done a very good re-creation of his style. It is, in our opinion, an original story and you should consider publishing it under your own name.

Yours etc.

The old man would have enjoyed the joke.